Shock flashed through Matilda St George's lovely gray eyes, along with a certain amount of fear, and there was an instant where a deep part of Enzo regretted that fear, remembering how it had felt when she'd looked at him with nothing but desire.

But then that instant was gone.

Good. She should be afraid. She should be *very* afraid.

Because he'd never been so furious.

Not that he would ever hurt her—he'd never hurt a woman in all his life and he wasn't about to start now. Still, he certainly wasn't about to make things easier for her.

He could forgive her for walking out on him that morning after their weekend together, even though the way she'd left, without even having the decency to say goodbye to his face, had been cowardly in the extreme.

He could even forgive her for the desire he still felt running through him, thick and hot as lava, despite the four years that had passed.

But what he couldn't forgive was that she hadn't told him about his son.

Because that boy *was* his son. Of that he had no doubt at all.

Secret Heirs of Billionaires

There are some things money can't buy...

Living life at lightning pace, these magnates are no strangers to stakes at their highest. It seems they've got it all... That is, until they find out that there's an unplanned item to add to their list of accomplishments!

Achieved:

1. Successful business empire.

2. Beautiful women in their bed.

3. *An heir to bear their name?*

Though every billionaire needs to leave his legacy in safe hands, discovering a secret heir shakes up the carefully orchestrated plan in more ways than one!

Uncover their secrets in:

The Secret Kept from the Italian by Kate Hewitt

Demanding His Secret Son by Louise Fuller

The Sheikh's Secret Baby by Sharon Kendrick

The Sicilian's Secret Son by Angela Bissell

Claimed for the Sheikh's Shock Son by Carol Marinelli

Shock Heir for the King by Clare Connelly

Look out for more stories in the
Secret Heirs of Billionaires series coming soon!

Jackie Ashenden

———

DEMANDING HIS HIDDEN HEIR

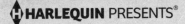
HARLEQUIN PRESENTS®

Recycling programs
for this product may
not exist in your area.

ISBN-13: 978-1-335-47844-3

Demanding His Hidden Heir

First North American publication 2019

Copyright © 2019 by Jackie Ashenden

Printed in U.S.A.

Jackie Ashenden writes dark, emotional stories with alpha heroes who've just gotten the world to their liking only to have it blown apart by their kick-ass heroines. She lives in Auckland, New Zealand, with her husband, the inimitable Dr. Jax, two kids and two rats. When she's not torturing alpha males and their gutsy heroines she can be found drinking chocolate martinis, reading anything she can lay her hands on, wasting time on social media or being forced to go mountain biking with her husband. To keep up-to-date with Jackie's new releases and other news, sign up to her newsletter at jackieashenden.com.

This is Jackie's stunning debut for Harlequin Presents—we hope you enjoy it!

Books by Jackie Ashenden

Harlequin Dare

The Knights of Ruin

Ruined
Destroyed

Kings of Sydney

King's Price
King's Rule
King's Ransom

Visit the Author Profile page
at Harlequin.com for more titles.

To discussions about fairy tales that can lead
to all sorts of good things...

CHAPTER ONE

Enzo Cardinali was not a man who appreciated parties. They were, in his opinion, nothing more than an excuse for people to waste time talking about trivialities while drinking themselves insensible and generally behaving badly.

He was not a fan of trivialities or bad behaviour either.

He stood in the corner of Henry St George's lavishly appointed drawing room, watching all the gorgeously attired people in it laugh and bray and talk nonsense to each other, nursing the same tumbler of Scotch he'd been holding for the past hour, impatient and not a little irritable.

The house party he'd been invited to had gone on for what seemed like an eternity and he was done with it. He'd been done with it the moment he'd arrived. His usual state of being, in other words.

He had no tolerance for waiting and, since other people didn't move at the speed he did, it felt as if waiting was all he did. Which made him constantly irritable.

Dante, his brother, had often told him he needed to cultivate a little patience, but Enzo didn't see why he should. He hadn't been put on this earth to make other people comfortable and, if they couldn't keep up with him, that was their problem. Of course, that then made it *his* problem and that was the part he didn't like.

He should have had Dante handle the particular bit of business he was in England for, but at the last minute he'd decided it was too important to let his laid-back brother handle it and so here he was. At a weekend-long house party at St George's extensive stately home deep in the Cotswolds.

St George was a rich industrialist with deep pockets and a taste for old-fashioned parties, during which he conducted most of his business. A state of affairs with which Enzo was not particularly happy. However, he was putting up with it because St George also owned an island just off the coast of Naples that Enzo was desperate to get his hands on.

So far the party had been useful, in that he was halfway to convincing the old man to sell the island to him, and now all he needed was to close the deal.

Except St George was baulking—for what reason, Enzo didn't know, nor did he care. What he cared about was having to exert himself and make nice, something that didn't come easy to him, in order to close the deal this weekend.

Across the room St George's white head bent as he leaned down to listen to a woman at his elbow. He was apparently a popular host and many of London's business elite jockeyed to get invites to his house parties.

Enzo shifted restlessly on his feet. *Dio*, this was interminable. He'd been waiting for an opportune moment to corner St George and present him with a final offer, but the man was constantly surrounded by people.

Dante had warned Enzo to be polite about it, but maybe his brother could go to hell.

Enzo wanted that island, Isola Sacra. It was the closest thing to Monte Santa Maria he'd come across, the tiny island kingdom in the Adriatic that had once been his home before his father, the king, had made one petty power play too many and parliament had decided it had had enough of royalty, declaring itself a republic and politely inviting the royal family to leave. For good.

The Cardinalis had found a place for themselves on mainland Italy, in Milan, but it had never felt like home to Enzo. He'd been fifteen when they'd left Monte Santa Maria and he'd felt rootless ever since.

Once, he'd been heir to a kingdom. Now, he had nothing.

Well, nothing except a multi-billion-dollar property development company, but that wasn't quite the same.

It was a home he wanted. And, since he could never go back to the one he'd had, he needed to find himself another somewhere else.

The guests in the drawing room swirled, the

laughter and noise putting him on edge, making him feel even more restless.

St George was still talking to that woman and Enzo decided that, if he hadn't finished talking to her in another couple of minutes, he was going to go over there and make St George an offer regardless of politeness. His brother's advice be damned.

He wasn't a stateless fifteen-year-old boy cowering in an apartment in Milan any more. He was the CEO of a billion-dollar company with offices in cities around the globe.

He might not have a country, but as far as the business world was concerned he was still a king.

Across the room the door opened suddenly, the movement catching Enzo's attention, and a small child peered round it, scanning the room with wide eyes.

Enzo frowned. What was a child doing up at this time of night? It was nearly eleven p.m.

The child—a small boy—took a step into the room, looking around uncertainly. He wore blue pyjamas and his black hair was spiked up. There was something familiar about him. Something that Enzo couldn't quite put his finger on.

The boy had to be St George's young son—a surprise late-in-life baby, since St George was in his early sixties. He'd married a woman around half his age four years ago and her subsequent pregnancy so soon after the wedding had caused a minor sensation.

Not that Enzo had ever been particularly interested in gossip, and why he remembered it now was anyone's guess.

But still. There was something about that boy.

The child took another few steps into the room, his eyes wide. They were an unusual colour. Gold. Like new-minted coins.

The familiarity tugged harder at Enzo. There weren't many people with eyes that colour, not so clear and startling. In fact, he only knew of two: his father and himself. Golden eyes were a Cardinali family trait and in Monte Santa Maria they'd traditionally been a sign of royalty.

Strange that this child should have them too, though obviously a coincidence.

There was another movement by the door and it opened wider this time, another figure standing in the doorway. A woman.

She wasn't dressed in high-end couture like the other guests, just a simple pair of jeans and a loose dark blue T-shirt. Her hair was piled up on top of her head in a messy bun, and it was as red as a fire against a twilight sky.

The tug of familiarity became a pull, deep and hard.

Her hair lying soft across his chest, a silken rope between his fingers as he'd pulled her towards him. Red as that hot mouth he'd kissed...

The woman scanned the room, giving him a good look at her face. High forehead and a sharp nose, a pointed, determined little chin. Freckles across her equally sharp cheekbones. Freckles that she'd fussed about in the tropical sun. Freckles scattered like gold dust across the luscious curves of her breasts, and he'd kissed every single one...

No. It couldn't be.

She gave the room another scan and then, as inevitably as the sun rising, her gaze met his and he found himself staring into eyes the colour of storm clouds and ice, a pure, clear grey that belied the passion that burned inside her.

A passion he'd tasted for more hours than he cared to count.

A passion he'd never felt before or since.

A passion that had gone as cold as ashes the morning he'd woken up in the villa to find she'd gone.

Four years ago, on an island in the Caribbean, at his brother's new resort, he'd met a woman.

A woman with red hair and freckles who'd turned him inside out. Who'd made him so hungry he hadn't been able to think straight.

Who'd made him forget, just for a couple of days, the constant ache in his heart for what he'd lost.

And who'd left him without even a goodbye.

Her gaze went wide as it met his, blanking with shock, and he knew instantly that, yes, it was her. The red-headed, passionate woman he'd had a two-day fling with four years ago.

He'd tried to forget her. *Dio*, he'd even convinced himself that he had.

But as she stared at him with those wide grey eyes, and he felt the burn of a sudden physical hunger, he knew that he'd been lying to himself.

He hadn't forgotten. Not the passion that had consumed them or the sense of homecoming that had come over him when she'd put her arms around him.

Or the fury when he'd woken up two days later, alone. His bed empty. His sheets cold.

The fury hit him again now, a hard punch to his gut, twisting with the hunger to become something so intense and volatile he could hardly breathe through it.

Four years, he'd dreamed of her. Four years, he'd woken up hard and aching, wanting something that all the money in the world couldn't buy him.

Something that only she had been able to give him.

He hadn't gone looking for her; he'd been too proud, telling himself that one woman would do as well as any other, but that was a lie and he knew it.

And now here she was, years later and thousands of miles from their island, standing in the doorway of an Englishman's drawing room and staring at him as if what was happening to him was happening to her too.

What was she doing here? Where had she been?

He'd taken one unconscious step towards her when the child turned around suddenly and said, 'Mummy.' And launched himself towards the doorway, running to her and wrapping his arms around her legs.

Enzo stopped dead as another punch of shock hit him.

Mummy.

The woman—Summer, she'd told him her name was—put her hand on the boy's head, but that smoky-grey gaze remained pinned to Enzo's. As if she couldn't look away.

That was St George's child wrapping his arms around her legs. St George's child, calling her 'Mummy'. Which meant...

She's St George's wife.

The shock got wider, deeper, spreading out inside him.

It shouldn't matter who she was. It shouldn't mean a thing. He shouldn't care, not after all this time.

He hadn't wanted to visit Dante's resort anyway. He'd just lost his first attempt at buying Isola Sacra after someone had bought it from under him, and the very last thing he'd felt like doing was checking up on a potential management issue on Dante's behalf.

But his brother hadn't been able to do it himself because of various commitments and Enzo was control-freak enough not to want to leave it to someone else.

He'd hated it the moment he'd got off the plane. There had been something about the dense tropical air and the brilliant blue of the sea that had crawled beneath his skin and unsettled him. Made him remember the land he'd come from and the home he hadn't been able to forget.

He'd stood underneath the palms, listening to the resort manager catalogue the problems the resort had been having, sweating in his custom-made suit, his hand-made leather shoes full of sand, restless and impatient to be home.

And then he'd seen her, a pale, curvy woman in a bright-red bikini that somehow matched her hair. She was on her way to the pool, a towel around her shoulders and a book in one hand, and she'd glanced at him as she'd walked past. She'd had the body of a fifties pin-up and a mouth made for sin, and it had curved as her gaze had met his. And that in itself had caught him by the throat.

Because people didn't look him in the eye—they were too afraid of him. But she had. In fact, there had even been a certain amusement in her gaze, as if she hadn't seen the icy, powerful CEO that everyone else saw. The ruthless king of business he'd turned himself into.

It was as if she'd seen the man he was underneath instead.

It had suddenly made his trousers feel two sizes too tight.

He hadn't thought twice about breaking off his conversation with the resort manager and following her to the pool.

She'd already settled herself on the lounger and, when he'd approached her, she'd given him a cool look from over the top of her book.

It hadn't remained cool for long.

Electricity had crackled in the air as their eyes had met and an hour later he'd been in her villa, his suit on the floor along with her bikini.

He'd had her against the wall that first time, fast

and hard, no time for niceties. There had only been desperation for them both. She'd gasped as he'd pushed inside her, and she'd felt so hot and tight, her silky thighs wrapped around his waist. Incredible. Her eyes had gone dark as they'd met his, and there had been no fear in them whatsoever. Only wonder. As if she'd never seen anything like him before in her entire life. Nothing had ever turned him on more. And then that wonder had fractured into pleasure as he'd begun to move inside her, driving her against the wall, driving them both into insanity...

Two days they'd had. Two days when he'd touched and tasted every inch of her, when he'd held her in his arms and shared things he'd never shared with another person before; had given her pieces of his soul that he'd never shared with anyone else.

And he'd thought that maybe he'd been mistaken when he'd thought home could be a place. That, maybe, home could be a person too.

Until she'd left him without a word.

No, it shouldn't matter. *She* shouldn't matter.

'Matilda?' St George finally ended his conversation with the woman to whom he'd been talking, his craggy face turning puzzled. 'Is there anything wrong?'

And the redhead—his Summer—finally tore her gaze from his to look at St George. 'N-no,' she said in that familiar smoky voice, the one that had turned husky when he'd been deep inside her. Or when his mouth had been between her thighs. Or when his hands had cupped her breasts, her skin silky against his palms. 'Simon woke up and got out of bed.' She bent and scooped the little boy up into her arms. 'I think he wandered in here by mistake.'

Matilda. Her name was Matilda. And she was St George's wife.

Enzo stood there, frozen, as St George came over to her and bent to the boy in her arms, murmuring something to him. The child turned his head to his father, but for a second looked over St George's shoulder, his bright golden gaze meeting Enzo's.

And realisation hit Enzo like a skyscraper falling.

Matilda St George was Summer, the island fling whose ghost had haunted him for four long, lonely years.

And really, even apart from the timing, there was only one way a child could have eyes that colour.

Enzo's fist tightened on his tumbler and a crack ran down the side of the glass.

That boy wasn't St George's.

That boy was his.

Matilda held Simon tightly as Henry murmured to him, her heart beating so fast and so loud she couldn't hear anything else.

She'd made a mistake. She'd made a *terrible* mistake.

She'd thought she'd been so clever, making sure she'd avoided him the whole weekend—going on a couple of day trips and then in the evenings keeping both Simon and herself to the upper levels of the house away from the guests.

There had only been tonight to get through and she'd been congratulating herself on how well that had worked out, Simon in bed early and herself curled up in bed too, watching a movie and eating ice-cream.

Forgetting all about the one guest she must avoid at all costs.

And then Simon had woken up and, because he liked people very much, the sounds coming from the drawing room had been irresistible.

Too concerned with finding her son, Matilda hadn't noticed the man in the corner at first. She'd given the room a quick scan, spotted nothing and had taken a step further into it before she'd recognised the crackle of electricity that had suddenly hummed over her skin.

A horribly familiar electricity.

So she'd stopped. And she'd looked. And there he'd been, standing near the sofa. So impossible to miss, she wondered how she hadn't seen him the first time.

Impossibly tall, impossibly broad. Radiating the same fierce, kinetic energy she remembered from years ago, all impatience, restlessness and heat.

He was dressed in a perfectly tailored suit of dark charcoal and his ink-black hair was cut ruthlessly short, highlighting those aristocratic cheekbones and the strong, sharp line of his jaw, the long blade of his nose and the carved sensuality of his mouth. A beautiful face, intensely compelling. Predatory, fierce and utterly unforgettable.

But it was his eyes that had caught her, held her. Making her freeze in place right where she'd stood.

Bright, burning gold. Like the tropical sun on an island years ago and full of the same searing heat.

Now a shudder coursed through her, a fire inside her that had long been cold suddenly bursting into flame. And, helplessly, she found herself glancing at him again, just to be sure it was actually him. As if the instant response of her body hadn't been enough.

But his attention wasn't on her this time. He was looking at Simon. And she had one second to think that perhaps he wouldn't notice the colour of her son's eyes, then his gaze lifted to hers once more.

And the weight of his fury descended on her.

He knows.

Henry was still talking but Matilda had long since ceased to listen. The fight or flight response had kicked in and all she could think about was getting out of the drawing room and away from the man she could still feel staring at her.

The man with whom she'd spent two intoxicating days.

The man from whom she'd run without even a goodbye.

The man who'd fathered the boy she held in her arms.

She felt strangely hot and cold at the same time, a bit sick too, and it was all she could do not to jerk away from Henry and run from the room there and then. But he wasn't one for public fusses so she stayed until he'd soothed Simon. Then, before he could do anything else, such as introduce her to his guests, she took her son and fled.

Back upstairs, Matilda tried to calm her frantically beating heart and attempted not to think about the man and the fury in his golden eyes. About how he'd taken a step towards her and how he'd stopped dead as Simon had run to her.

And most especially she tried not to think about that flare of heat deep inside her the moment his gaze had met hers, or the ache that had gripped her, an ache she'd tried all these years to forget in an attempt to put it behind her.

A futile attempt, as it turned out.

She put Simon back into his bed and tucked him in, singing him one of the lullabies he used to like as a baby. Then she stroked his back until he drifted off.

After making sure he was definitely asleep this time, Matilda moved out of his room and shut the door gently. Then she leaned her back against the wall in the hallway outside, put her shaking hands over her face and quietly allowed herself to freak out.

She'd seen the guest list, obviously, had noticed his name, and she'd idly asked Henry why he'd invited some Italian billionaire to the party. Because the man wanted to buy some island that Henry owned, or something to that effect. Matilda hadn't really been listening.

She'd still been struggling with her shock at seeing his name on the list.

Enzo Cardinali. Billionaire property developer and heir to a kingdom that no longer existed. A cold, ruthless, driven businessman who, along with his brother Dante, had taken Cardinal Construction, a small construction start-up, and turned it into Cardinal Enterprises, a huge multi-national that had expanded beyond building houses and into property development as well as various other industries. Hotels. Real estate. Manufacturing. Technology.

He was well known in the kind of *Fortune 500* circles Henry also moved in, and had a reputation for being an icy force of nature, both feared and respected for the ruthless way he did business. He was a shark, a cold-blooded predator through and through—or at least, that was what the articles she'd read about him all said.

Not that she'd read a lot of articles. But she did like to keep up with what he was doing every now and then. It always paid to know the direction from which any potential threats might come.

Except he hadn't been a threat four years ago on that island. And he'd been neither cold-blooded or ruthless.

He'd burned like the sun and she, utterly defenceless against a man like him, had burned along with him.

She gave a little moan, the wall pressing hard against her back, the urge simply to slide down it and sit on the expensive Turkish runner that covered the floor almost overwhelming.

Why had she thought it wouldn't be a problem?

Why had she believed that she could easily avoid him? Why hadn't she taken Simon and gone away to visit her aunt and uncle for the weekend? Or gone to London, or basically gone *anywhere* else?

But there wasn't any point thinking about the whys and what ifs. She hadn't gone anywhere. She'd stayed and he'd seen her. And, worse, he'd seen Simon.

He knows.

Of course he did. There was no disguising the colour of her son's eyes. So different. So unique. So beautiful.

A family trait, or so Enzo had told her one night as they'd lain curled up on the beach in each other's arms looking at the stars, and he'd told her about the island kingdom to which he'd once been heir.

There had been a warmth to him that, after living with her emotionally distant aunt and uncle, had felt like walking into summer after long years of winter. It had been irresistible to her, so intensely attractive, she'd given herself to him without thought.

She'd been on that island for one last holiday before her official engagement, a gift from Henry, who'd known all along that she hadn't wanted to marry him but who'd been trying to make it easier for her. Not that she'd known it at the time. All she'd understood was that, if she didn't marry Henry, her aunt and uncle would lose their beautiful stately home deep in the Devonshire countryside.

It had been a very English, almost mediaeval arrangement.

After the death of her parents when she'd been seven, she'd been taken in by her childless uncle and aunt, and although they'd distantly been kind to her she'd never managed to get rid of the feeling that she was only there on sufferance. That they'd been forced to take her.

So she'd tried to make herself useful. Tried to be no bother. Her uncle didn't like fusses or distractions, so she'd kept herself quiet and tried to behave herself, not put a foot out of line. She hadn't wanted them to get rid of her or regret giving her a home.

And it had all worked very well.

So well that, when her aunt and uncle had been refused more money by the bank for the upkeep of their house and their family friend Henry St George had stepped in, offering money in return for marriage to Matilda, they'd naturally assumed she'd agree.

And she had. Because they'd taken her in, had given her a home and sacrificed the later years of their lives bringing her up. Marrying Henry St George so they could keep their house had seemed a small sacrifice to make in return.

That she actually hadn't wanted to marry Henry, she'd kept quiet about. He was her aunt and uncle's age and, even though he was a nice enough man, she hadn't been in love with him. She hadn't been even attracted to him. He'd told her that he didn't require sex in the marriage, that all he wanted was companionship in his later years, yet Matilda had still been apprehensive about it.

So when Henry had offered her a holiday by herself at a Caribbean resort before the engagement—a kind of last hurrah as a single woman—she'd decided to take it as a treat for herself.

And that was when she'd met him.

Enzo.

He'd been talking to the resort manager as she'd been on her way to the pool, dressed—rather improbably, given the fact that they were on a tropical island—in a three-piece suit.

He should have looked ridiculous, standing there in the hot sun dressed in layers of fine Italian wool. But he hadn't. He'd looked dark, commanding and fierce. And utterly, devastatingly, gorgeous.

She'd never bothered much with men, preferring to stick to her studies at school, and then her English degree at university, but Enzo Cardinali had been a man completely outside her experience.

She hadn't been able to take her eyes off him.

And then he'd looked at her, that intense, amber gaze slamming into hers, stealing her breath, stealing her thought.

She'd led a fairly sheltered life since she'd gone to live with her aunt and uncle, keeping to the straight and narrow, never having put a foot wrong. But there was something about this man that had reached right down inside her and woken a part of herself that she'd put on ice the day her parents had died.

An angry, hot, rebellious part.

He'd looked furious, standing there in the sun,

and in the heated gold of his eyes she'd seen a challenge. So she'd answered it.

She'd smiled and arched an eyebrow, met him stare for stare as she'd walked past, every cell of her being suddenly alive and aware, thrilled at her own daring.

It had been like poking a tiger in a cage, safe in the knowledge that she wouldn't get eaten because of the bars, yet still having the wild adrenaline rush of baiting such a dangerous creature.

But she hadn't thought he'd bother following her until he'd suddenly appeared in the pool area. Every eye in the place had been drawn to his electric presence as he'd strode towards her lounger. But he'd ignored them all.

His focus had been entirely on her.

And the good girl she'd been since her parents' death had burned to ash right there and then.

Back at the villa, he'd kissed her as soon as the door had closed, his mouth hot, demanding and desperate. She'd been overwhelmed. The only kisses she'd ever had had been from one shy boy back in school at a dance and they'd been nothing— *nothing*—compared to the hard mastery of Enzo's mouth.

He'd pushed her against the wall and she'd let him, her heartbeat like a drum in her head, hoping like hell he wouldn't notice her inexperience and leave, because more than anything she didn't want him to go.

But he'd given no sign of noticing anything but the chemistry burning out of control between them.

He'd ripped the bikini from her body, leaving her no time for shyness or nerves. No time for second guessing. And then his large, warm hands had been on her, cupping her bare breasts, teasing her nipples with his thumbs…

Matilda gave another soft groan, pressing her hands harder against her closed lids, the memory in her head replaying no matter how much she didn't want it to.

All she'd been able to hear was her own frantic breathing and the soft gasp that had escaped her as his hand had slid lower, down between her thighs to where she'd been aching and wet. His fingers had glided over her slick flesh, sending sharp, electric bolts of pleasure through her, making her shudder and arch against the wall.

No one had ever touched her there before, not in her entire life, and she hadn't been able to believe she was letting a man she'd only just met do it then. But she had. And it had felt illicit, thrilling and so unbelievably good…

She let out a sharp breath, forcing the memories away and ignoring the subtle throb between her thighs.

No, she couldn't think of that. The woman she'd been on that island wasn't her any more, and she didn't want to be that woman anyway. Not these days. Not now she was a mother with responsibilities.

When she'd returned to England, she'd worked hard to fit herself back into the good-girl box. She'd married Henry like she'd promised she would and put her studies on hold so she could care for Simon. It hadn't been so bad.

She hadn't found out she'd was pregnant until four months into her marriage, but luckily by then she'd realised that Henry truly had meant it when he'd said that he only wanted friendship. He'd been good to her, drying her tears when she'd confessed about her pregnancy, and deciding to save them both a scandal by claiming Simon as his own. He'd never asked for the name of Simon's father and she'd never volunteered it.

He'd been a good man and a kind husband.

But she really, *really* wished that he hadn't invited Enzo Cardinali to his stupid house party.

She swallowed and let some of the tension bleed out of her. God, what a mess. Still, it wasn't all bad. The party ended tonight and tomorrow everyone would be gone, including Enzo, with any luck.

She'd never have to see or think about him again.

You really think he's going to let Simon go now he knows?

Dread rose inside her because she knew the answer to that.

Of course he wouldn't.

The quality of the silence changed abruptly in the hallway, and all the hairs on the back of her neck rose.

Slowly, carefully, her heartbeat going double-time, Matilda lowered her hands from her face.

And found Enzo Cardinali standing right in front of her.

'*Buono notte*, Mrs St George,' he said in that deep voice she knew so well, the one that had once been full of heat and yet now was so cold. 'I think you and I need to have a little chat.'

CHAPTER TWO

SHOCK FLASHED THROUGH Matilda St George's lovely grey eyes, along with a certain amount of fear, and there was an instant where a deep part of him regretted that fear, remembering how it had felt when she'd looked at him with nothing but desire.

But then that instant was gone.

Good. She should be afraid. She should be *very* afraid.

Because he'd never been so furious.

Not that he would ever hurt her—he'd never hurt a woman in all his life and he wasn't about to start now. Still, he certainly wasn't about to make things easy for her.

He could forgive her for walking out on him that morning after their weekend together, even though the way she'd left, without even having had the decency to say goodbye to his face, had been cowardly in the extreme.

He could even forgive her for the desire he still felt running through him, thick and hot as lava, despite the four years that had passed.

But what he couldn't forgive was that she hadn't told him about his son.

Because that boy *was* his son. Of that he had no doubt at all.

Her eyes widened as they stared up into his, her pale throat moving convulsively. Her pulse was beating fast and hard at the base of her throat and he couldn't seem to take his eyes off it.

It had beat like that for him when he'd first touched her. Getting fast, then faster. Out of control as he'd bent his head to taste it…

'A chat?' she said huskily, her chin firming, the shock and fear in her gaze quickly masked. 'A chat about what?'

With an effort, Enzo dragged his gaze from her throat.

So, she was going to pretend she didn't know what he was talking about, was she? Well, unfortunately for her, he wasn't having it.

'I'm not here to play games with you, Summer,' he said coldly. 'Or should I say *Matilda*. I'm here to talk about my son.'

Another burst of quicksilver emotion flashed in her eyes, then it was gone, nothing but a cool wall of grey in its place. 'Yes, that's my name. You don't have to say it like a pantomime villain. And as to a son… Well.' Her chin came up. 'I don't know what you're talking about.'

The challenge made his anger flare hot at the same time as the physical hunger inside him tightened.

The blue cotton of her T-shirt was loose but the

quickened way she was breathing made the fabric pull across the generous curves of her breasts. And he was very aware of how close she was, of how warm she was.

Which only made him angrier. He didn't know why this chemistry between them was still burning the way it was, but it needed to stop.

She'd taken his son and there was nothing more important than that.

'Is that how you're going to play this?' He didn't bother to temper the acid in his tone. 'You're going to pretend you don't know anything about that child you just rescued downstairs? The child with eyes the same colour as mine?' He took a step towards her. 'Perhaps you're going to pretend that you don't know who I am either.'

She held her ground, even though she didn't have anywhere to go, not when there was a wall behind her. 'No, of course not.' Her gaze didn't flicker. 'I know who you are, Enzo Cardinali.'

The sound of his name in her soft, husky voice made a bolt of lightning shoot straight down his spine, helplessly reminding him of other times when she'd said it.

Such as on the daybed of the villa, when he'd been deep inside her and her legs had been wrapped around his waist. Or out beside the private pool, on the sun lounger, where he'd spent a long time tasting her, his name echoing off all those tiled surfaces, drowning out the sound of the waves of the beach beyond.

She'd turned him inside out, made him think that perhaps there was more to him than the ruthless, selfish businessman he'd always accepted he was. A man more like his father than he should have been comfortable with.

That perhaps he was something else, something better.

Only to have that hope ripped away by her disappearing the next day.

He'd searched the resort for her, thinking that maybe she'd simply gone to the pool, the gym or the restaurant. But she hadn't been in any of those places. She hadn't been anywhere. And it hadn't been until a good hour later that he'd come back from his search and realised that all her belongings had gone.

She'd left the island entirely.

He hadn't chased her. It had been her choice to leave and so he'd let her go. There were plenty of other women he could find the same kind of release with; after all, it wasn't as if he had a shortage.

He'd been wrong to think that perhaps he was a different man. Wrong to believe that she was special. He wasn't different, she wasn't special and he was done with her.

Except right now, with her standing in front of him—those soft red curls falling around her face and with the way that T-shirt draped reminding him of how the silky curves of her breasts had felt in his palms—done was the last thing he felt.

It made him want to snarl at the same time as it

made him want to push her against the wall, pull those jeans off her, lift her up and sink into the tight wet heat that he'd never been able to forget.

'Good.' He kept his voice hard, trying not to let the heat creep into it. 'Then if you know who I am you can explain to me why you didn't tell me that I have a son.'

She was already pale; now she went the colour of ashes. But that defiant slant to her chin remained, the expression in her eyes guarded. 'Like I said, I don't know what you're talking about.'

Enzo's rage, already inflamed by his body's betrayal, curdled into something very close to incandescence and it burned like fire in his blood, thick and hot.

He'd never been so angry in all his life, some distant part of him vaguely appalled at the intensity of his emotions—a reminder that he needed to lock it down, since his iron control was the only thing that set him apart from his power-hungry father.

But in this moment he didn't care.

This woman, this beautiful, sexy, infuriating woman, hadn't told him he had a son and, more, she'd kept it from him for four years.

Four. Years.

He took another step towards her, unable to help himself, the heat in his veins so hot it felt as if it was going to ignite him where he stood. 'I see. So you *are* going to pretend you know nothing. How depressingly predictable of you.'

'Simon is *my* son.' Her hands had gone into fists

at her sides and she didn't move, not an inch. 'And H-Henry's.' Her gaze was as cool as winter rain, but that slight stutter gave her away.

'No.' Enzo kept his voice honed as a steel blade. 'He is not. Those eyes are singular to the Cardinali line. Which makes him mine.'

'But I—'

'How long have you known, *Matilda*? A year? Two?' He took another step, forcing her back against the wall. 'Or did you know the moment you returned to England? With my seed inside you? Come to think of it, is that why you married him? Because you were ashamed? Because you didn't want my son to be a bastard? Did you think he would make a better father than I would?'

Fear flickered through her expression like lightning through clouds at the relentless barrage of questions, but he wasn't sorry.

He was only inches away from her now, the heat of her body and the subtle scent of jasmine suddenly filling his senses. A familiar sweetness. He remembered how it had mixed with the musk of her arousal, making him hard almost instantly.

Dio, it was making him hard now.

He tried to control it the way he controlled all parts his life because, really, his responses seemed disproportionate. Especially considering that children had never been part of his plan, or at least not immediately. He'd wanted to find a home first before he settled down with a family.

But now he had a son. A *son*. A child he'd never

known existed and would never have known about if he hadn't come to this house party. If the boy hadn't wandered into that room at that very moment.

Enzo was a king with no kingdom. His inheritance had been denied him, his birth right taken from him. His mother had walked out not long after they'd left Monte Santa Maria, taking Dante with her, leaving Enzo alone with his bitter, enraged father. A father who'd then ignored his existence. Both parents had since died and, though he didn't mourn them, they'd taken his history with them. And, despite the fact that he still had his brother and his billion-dollar company, it wasn't enough. It had never been enough.

But now he had a child and this child was his. A part of him in a way that nothing and no one else could ever be, and he was furious—no, he was *enraged*—that she'd even entertained the possibility that she could keep him from the child.

If she recognised his anger she either didn't let it get to her or she dismissed it, because even backed up against the wall she gave him nothing but cool self-possession. 'Simon is Henry's. Like I told you. And that's all there is to it.'

Oh, no, she wasn't doing that. Not when the truth of it was so easy to spot a blind man could have seen it.

Enzo put a hand on the wall at one side of her silky red head and leaned in close so she had no choice but to stare straight at him. 'Look at me, *cara*. Look at me and tell me that you don't see your son staring back.'

Her gaze flickered as it met his and, as he watched, her pupils dilated. Her breathing had got faster and he could hear the slight hitch in it.

The air around them grew dense, heavy.

She was looking at him the way he remembered. The way she had when he'd been deep in her wet heat and her thighs had been wrapped tight around him, as if she'd been starving for something only he could give her.

So, she wasn't as cool and self-possessed as she seemed.

And he wasn't the only one who felt this.

This is a mistake. Step back.

But he couldn't move. Couldn't look away. There was nothing but satisfaction inside him and a certain kind of male triumph. Even after all these years, even after she'd married another man, she still wanted him.

All he had to do to kiss her would be to lower his head just a little and that perfect red mouth would be in reach.

Yes—married, remember? To someone who is not you.

At that moment she blinked, as if she'd remembered the very same thing, and the glazed expression in her eyes vanished. 'Mr Cardinali,' she said with only the faintest trace of huskiness. 'I must insist that you—'

'The island. The villa,' he interrupted because, even with the reminder that she had a husband, apparently he still couldn't help himself. 'You, naked on the daybed beside the window. You, naked on the floor just inside the door. Me inside you. Come, now, don't you remember?'

She flushed a deep, fascinating red. 'I don't know what—'

'Remember when I took you so hard you thought we'd broken the bed?' There was a devil inside him, wanting to push her, or maybe simply to punish her. 'But we hadn't. The only thing that broke was the condom. I told you we'd deal with it in the morning. But in the morning, you were gone.'

Her flush became even deeper, matching her hair. Making her eyes glow silver. She'd looked exactly like that in his arms those two nights he'd had with her, burning like a flame, just as hungry as he was, just as desperate.

And he knew he shouldn't get any closer, but he couldn't stop himself from putting the other hand on the wall on the other side of her head, caging her between his palms. 'You got pregnant,' he went on, rage and desire burning a hole inside him. 'And you didn't tell me. You didn't even bother to send a message. No, you went ahead and married another man and let *him* claim *my* son.'

She was very still, her jaw tight, her chest rising and falling fast and hard. Another couple of inches and the tips of her breasts would be brushing up against his chest. And he'd stake all his money on the fact that her nipples would be hard. He remembered how sensitive she was there.

'Come any closer and I'll scream for help,' she said tautly.

He gave a short, hard laugh. It would be so easy to push. To put his mouth to her throat, taste that frantically beating pulse and see whether she'd *really* scream for help or whether she'd just scream. For him.

But she wasn't his. And he wasn't that desperate.

'Oh, don't worry. I wouldn't dream of it. I only wanted to discuss what do about our son like civilised people, but I see you're not capable of that. Which unfortunately leaves me with no choice.' He shoved himself away from the wall, disturbed by how difficult it actually was to step away from her. 'If you continue to deny the truth staring us both in the face, I must insist on having a paternity test done. As soon as possible.'

Anger flickered through her fascinating eyes. 'I won't allow it. You can't—'

'I can,' he interrupted harshly. 'I will.'

'But Henry—' She stopped all of a sudden, as if she'd given herself away.

'But Henry what?' Enzo demanded, fighting the sudden need to reach down, take that determined little chin in his hand and hold it so she'd have to look at him. But touching her would definitely be a mistake so he clenched his hands into fists instead.

She bent her head, her reddish lashes sweeping down to hide her gaze, and raised a hand to her forehead, rubbing at it as if she had a headache.

If it had been at a different time and she a different woman, he a different man, he might have been sympathetic. But the time was now and she wasn't a different woman. And he wasn't different man.

She was the mother of his child, a child he'd had no idea even existed until now, which made sympathy the very last thing he felt towards her.

'Henry doesn't know,' she said at last, quietly, her attention still on the floor. 'He knows that Simon isn't his. He just…doesn't know that you're Simon's father.'

The triumph that went through him at the acknowledgement surprised him. Not that he needed it when the truth of the boy's parentage was so obvious. But there was something about *her* saying it that got to him, that made possessiveness turn over inside him.

He wanted to put his hand on her lovely throat, claim her the way he had years ago with a kiss. And more.

But she wasn't his and, as he already knew, he wasn't that man. Not any more.

Now the only thing he wanted was his son.

Ignoring the urge to touch her, he shoved his fists into his pockets instead. 'Well, that was easy.' He kept his voice hard, not giving anything away. 'Feels good to tell the truth, does it not? But tell me, Matilda, would you ever have admitted it to either of us if you hadn't seen me downstairs? Or would you have remained the coward you were when you ran out on me that morning?'

The wall at Matilda's back was the only thing holding her up. Or at least, given the current state of her knees, she was pretty certain it was the only thing holding her up. Certainly, if she'd taken even one step away from it, she probably would have fallen into a heap at Enzo Cardinali's expensively shod feet.

The questions he kept firing at her were like a thousand tiny cuts. Each one not so painful on its own but, thrown all at once and with such fury, they had the power to make her bleed.

And it didn't help that he was right. That he was entitled to every single ounce of his righteous anger.

Or that, apart from her son, he was the single most beautiful thing she'd ever seen in her life.

When he'd caged her against the wall, she'd thought she was going to catch fire right where she stood.

He'd been so close, radiating rage, those mesmerising golden eyes making her breath catch hard in her throat. Making her so aware of him she could feel it in every cell in her body. And, even though his deep, rough voice was frozen all the way through, the way his accent curled each word only deepened that awareness still further.

God, how she'd loved that accent of his. Loved how it had made the name she'd chosen for herself sound exotic, especially when she'd known she was anything but. And then the dialect of Italian that he'd whispered to her in the depths of the night, words she didn't understand, soft and lyrical as he'd touched her, as he'd moved inside her…

Matilda sucked in a silent breath, fighting the relentless pull of desire. But it was difficult.

Although he'd pushed himself away, it felt as if he was still close, the warm, spicy scent of his aftershave lingering, the heat of his body like a furnace in front of her.

Her heartbeat was loud in her ears, deafening her.

Henry had always told her that, as long as she kept everything out of the media, she could have lovers. He hadn't wanted to deprive her of sex if that was what she wanted. But she hadn't wanted. The passion she'd shared with Enzo had scared her for reasons she couldn't articulate, so she hadn't wanted to go there again. Not with anyone.

She'd thought it would be easy, that she wouldn't miss it but, now that Enzo himself was standing right in front of her, she realised that it hadn't been easy. And she *did* miss it. She missed *him*.

No, she couldn't do this with him. Not again. Not with Henry downstairs and Simon in his bedroom behind her.

Not even for herself this time.

Forcing the ache away, she made herself concentrate on the here and now, not the past, because she was in danger and so was her son. Not physical danger—Enzo would never hurt either of them; she knew that for truth—but she was wary of the emotional chasm that awaited her if she played this wrong.

And she'd already taken a misstep by denying him the truth. She didn't even know why she'd pretended she didn't know what he was talking about, only that she'd been scared. Frightened of how angry he was with her and how badly she wanted to justify herself and explain. But she had a horrible feeling all he'd see in her was excuses.

She had a horrible feeling that that was what she'd see in herself.

But she didn't want to think about that right now. If she got this wrong, he would more than likely try to take her son from her, and there was no way she was going to let that happen. She wasn't a particularly brave person, but Simon was hers. She'd lost her parents and her home and she wasn't about to lose anything more.

And if he wanted the truth? Well, she'd give it to him.

'Henry told me that he didn't need to know who Simon's father was,' she said, pleased with how steady her voice sounded. 'So I didn't tell him. And as for you…' She swallowed, clutching onto her bravery with everything she had, Enzo's furious stare making all the words clump together in her throat. 'I didn't know about the pregnancy until four months after I came back to England. And then I…took a while to figure out who you were because you didn't give me your last name.'

He was so tall. So full of indignant Italian fury. He made the air in the hallway around them crackle with the force of his anger. She could feel it pushing against her, wild electricity against her skin.

'I'm not that difficult to find, *cara*,' he said, dark and low, a caress down her spine. 'Easy enough if you have the will and the determination. If you really wanted to find me.'

'I did find you.' Her throat was dry, a sick feeling in her gut as she remembered how her hands had shaken as she'd punched in the number she'd found in the course of a web search. And how she'd felt like throwing up as the phone had rung and rung, because she'd never made a mistake so big before. 'And I called you. But you didn't answer. It was some other man. And, when I explained, he called me a liar and told me never to bother you again.'

'What man?' Enzo's eyes glittered. 'And that's all it took? Someone told you not to call so you didn't?'

'I don't know who he was,' she shot back, knowing it sounded weak, yet saying it anyway because it was the only defence she had. 'He didn't give me his name. And I…I thought you probably wouldn't remember me. And that you probably wouldn't want some inexperienced redhead showing up telling you that you were a father.'

She hadn't been able to bear that particular thought. Of finding him, only to have him either not recognise her or call her a liar the way the man on the phone had. Or both. And most especially not after what they'd shared on the island together. Where for once in her life she'd felt like someone had actually wanted her.

'I'm glad you could read my mind so easily.' Enzo's voice was heavy with sarcasm. 'From all the way over in England.'

She flushed, biting down on all the things she

wanted to say. Defensive things that only sounded hollow, like excuses. 'I'm sorry.' It came out stiff and stilted. 'I know I should have got in touch with you. There was no excuse for me not to. I just…'

Time had passed. And the longer she'd left it the harder it had become to pick up the phone. Until she'd decided that it was easier on both of them not to do it at all.

You're selfish. Just like your parents were.

Her uncle's voice floated through her head, angry and hurt, from the day she'd made that one, cursory protest about marrying Henry.

No, she wasn't selfish. She wasn't. She'd given up a lot to marry Henry. And she'd done it for them.

'If you think a sorry will cut it, you're sadly mistaken.' The fierce, predatory lines of Enzo's face were hard with anger. 'I can forgive you for walking out on me that morning without a word. But I will not forgive the four years I missed with my son.'

The thread of fear that had been winding round and round her pulled tight. There was no mercy in those beautiful golden eyes; none to be had in his handsome face either.

God, why hadn't she made sure Simon was asleep before creeping back to her room for ice-cream? Normally, she didn't allow herself to relax until he was. But she'd been feeling so…jittery.

So what are you going to do? Just give Simon up without a fight?

An unfamiliar determination filled her, crowding

out the fear, steeling her spine. No, there was no way in hell she'd do that. Bravery wasn't her strong suit but she couldn't bear not to fight for her son.

He might not have been what she'd planned, but there would never be a day when he wasn't wanted. When he wasn't loved. And she wouldn't give him up, not for anyone, still less some arrogant Italian who thought he was God.

No matter what history she might have had with said Italian.

She might once have run from Enzo. But she wasn't going to run now, not with Simon on the line.

Forcing the fear back, Matilda straightened against the wall. 'I'm not asking for forgiveness, Enzo. But for what it's worth, you have my—'

'Enough,' he interrupted brutally. 'Whatever it is you're offering, it is worth nothing.' The fire in his eyes blazed. 'There is only one thing I will accept from you—and make no mistake, Matilda, if you do not give it to me I *will* take it.'

The fear wrapped around her throat, strangling her. Because there could be only one thing he was talking about. Only one. And he was sleeping in the bedroom at her back.

No. *Hell*, no.

She'd moved in front of Simon's door before she'd even thought about it, her gaze meeting Enzo's head on. 'No,' she said, injecting every ounce of strength she had into the word. 'You'll take him over my dead body.'

Enzo hadn't moved a muscle and yet the sense of

threat he radiated filled the hallway around them, a pressure so intense she could hardly breathe.

'The child is mine,' he said, almost gently. 'And I will have him.'

Then, before Matilda could think of a reply, he turned and stalked off down the hallway.

CHAPTER THREE

ENZO'S FURY HAD crystallised into something hard and cold and lethal that glittered like the edge of a steel blade.

The way Matilda had gone to stand in front of Simon's door, as if she'd thought that Enzo would hurt him…

Dio, he'd thought it wasn't possible to be any more furious.

He was wrong.

First there had been her acknowledgement that she'd made only one attempt to contact him, an attempt that had been half-hearted at best. Then she'd admitted that she hadn't tried again after that because she'd thought he wouldn't remember her…

He couldn't understand how she could think that. How she could assume that he'd forget what had happened between them. That all those moments of intimacy, of connection, had been unimportant to him.

It didn't seem possible. What was more likely was that she was using that as an excuse for her own cowardice.

The very thought made him incandescent with rage, not helped by the fact that as he strode down the hallway he was still hard. For her.

He hadn't expected their chemistry still to be there, but it was. And just as strong as it had been all those years ago.

Perhaps stronger.

No. That was the rage talking. It had to be. Not that it made any difference whatsoever. No matter how badly he might want her, he wanted his son more. And she could make all the excuses in the world for her behaviour, but he was taking Simon, whether she liked it or not.

First, though, since this was St George's house and she was St George's wife, it was only fair that he inform the other man of his intentions. Not to mention the truth.

And Isola Sacra, the island you want to buy?

Ah, yes, that.

If he handled it right, maybe he could have both, his son and a place to take him. A place they could both call home.

Ignoring the pressure in his groin, he strode back into the drawing room, paying no attention to the crowd of people standing around St George this time.

The older man looked up as Enzo approached, but the expression on Enzo's face must have given him away because St George's ready smile faded. 'What can I do for you, Cardinali?' A frown creased his forehead. 'Is there something wrong?'

'I need to speak with you.' Enzo didn't bother

to make it anything but the order it very much was. 'Now, if you please.'

St George's expression flickered minutely, his mouth tightening. 'Of course. Come to my study.'

The English. They did so hate public unpleasantness. And unfortunately for St George things were about to get ten thousand times more unpleasant.

Curious stares followed them as St George led the way out of the drawing room, but Enzo ignored them. He didn't care what other people thought of him at the best of times and he cared even less now.

St George's study was decorated along very English aristocratic lines, with lots of wood panelling and tall bookshelves full of books that no one had read nor would ever read. A heavy oak desk stood in front of the window, a couple of red velvet armchairs positioned nearby. There was even a stag's head over the fireplace opposite and the usual ode to the glories of hunting in the form of paintings of horses and hounds on the walls.

Enzo hated it. He preferred clean lines and modernity, not an overcrowded, cluttered space like this one.

He paced over to the fire, antsy and restless as St George headed for the drinks cabinet, getting out the brandy.

'There's no need for that,' Enzo snapped, in no mood for niceties. 'This won't take long.'

St. George frowned and put down the decanter. 'And what is "this" all about, then?'

'Your son. Or rather, *my* son.'

A puzzled look appeared on the other man's face. 'I'm sorry? I'm not sure I follow.'

'Simon is not your son.' Enzo shoved his hands into his pockets in an effort to keep himself still. 'He's mine.'

There was a heavy silence.

A hard light gleamed in St George's dark-brown eyes. 'I think you'd better explain.'

'I spoke to your wife,' Enzo said coolly. 'She said that you know Simon isn't your son, but that she never told you who his father is. Well, I'm here to tell you that *I'm* his father. Four years ago she had an affair while on holiday at an island resort in the Caribbean. And she had that affair with me.'

St George said nothing, merely looked at him. Then he sighed heavily and glanced away, picking up the decanter again and pouring himself a hefty glass. 'Are you sure you don't want any?' he asked, waving the bottle in Enzo's direction. 'Seems like this is a conversation that will require it.'

'No,' Enzo said flatly. 'What I want is my son.'

St George took a large swallow of his drink. 'Took you long enough.'

'Excuse me?'

'Well, Simon is four now. That's a long time to leave a boy—'

'I didn't know,' Enzo interrupted, making no effort to temper the harsh note in his voice. 'Your lovely wife apparently didn't see fit to tell me she was pregnant.'

Another silence fell, even heavier than the last.

'Ah,' St George murmured. 'I see.'

'Yes, I'm sure you do. Now.' Enzo's hands clenched into fists in his pocket. 'The fact that I'm talking to you is purely a courtesy. Tomorrow I will be taking my son back to Milan.'

St George stiffened, his mouth opening as if to say something.

But at that point the door of the study opened and Matilda stood on the threshold, flushed and lovely, steel in her gaze.

Enzo wasn't surprised that she'd come after him, not after the way she'd protested about him taking Simon. No doubt she was here to stop him.

Well, she could try.

Matilda glanced at her husband then looked back at Enzo, and he knew that she'd realised what he'd done, because her eyes went silver with anger. 'You told him, didn't you?' she said in a low voice. 'You told my husband what—'

'Someone had to,' Enzo shot back, his fury igniting anew.

'It wasn't your place to do so.'

'I am Simon's father.' He said the words with a certain relish, liking the way her expression tightened at the sound of them. 'It is absolutely my place to do so. And, besides, I am a guest here and it is only polite that I let my host know that I will be taking Simon back to Italy with me in the morning.'

Shock flickered over her pointed face, closely followed by something bright and sharp that was probably pain.

And for a second that pain found an echo in himself, as if hurting her had hurt him as well. But he shoved that thought aside before it could find purchase.

He couldn't afford mercy or sympathy. He couldn't afford to be gentle.

His father had always told him that the softer emotions were useless in a king. That they undermined a man, hollowed him out, made him weak. Ruthlessness, strength and ice-cold determination were infinitely better.

Of course, his father wasn't exactly a great example to follow, not considering how his own ruthlessness had nearly beggared his country, not to mention nearly crushed his own wife; but, when life forced you down the same path, you had to take what advice you could get. Certainly that particular piece had helped Enzo grow his company into what it was today and he'd never seen any reason to change his approach.

Not even to spare this woman pain. Especially not *this* woman…

But, whatever hurt she'd felt, it was gone the next second, the colour of her eyes darkening into storm clouds as she strode straight up to him. 'No,' she said. 'You're not taking Simon anywhere.'

He stared down at her, trying to ignore the visceral thrill that gripped him at the way she challenged him. 'Oh, no? Just watch me.'

'You won't.' Her chin lifted. 'I won't allow it.'

The desire he'd been fighting caught at him yet

again. *Dio*, had she been like this on the island with him? Surely he would have remembered if she had. Because there was something about her opposition that he found intensely sexy. It made him want to fight her, push her. See what she was really made of.

She had a strength to her that he hadn't seen before, glimpses of an iron determination that equalled his own.

But of course. She was protecting her child.

He almost would have approved if he hadn't been the thing she was protecting his child from.

'You think you can stop me?' he growled.

'I think that ripping a child away from the only home he's ever known is criminal, so yes. Yes, I bloody well would.'

Her choice of words hit him in a place he shouldn't have been vulnerable, and certainly not these days.

Ripping a child away from the only home he's ever known...

It had been night when his father's bodyguards had woken him, dragging him and a still sleepy Dante from their beds and onto the boat that would take them from Monte Santa Maria and to the Italian mainland. They'd had no time to take anything with them, no time to say goodbye to their friends or the places they'd loved. It had taken twenty minutes to be ripped away from his home and everything he'd known, and two days later he'd found himself in a one-roomed apartment in Milan, his father raging at his 'ungrateful subjects', his mother pale and silent, saying nothing at all.

Could he really do the same thing to his own child? *Like your father did to you?*

His jaw was so tight it ached. No, he couldn't do what had been done to him, no matter how intensely he wanted to take his son and hold him fast. Keep him safe.

Selfishness had been a characteristic of his father's that he'd inherited, something his mother had flung in his face before she'd left, and he owned it. But right now Simon and what was best for him seemed more important.

And Matilda was right. He couldn't simply take the boy from everything that was familiar to him.

Unless…

The idea sat inside him, burning like a hot coal, the rightness of it making him wonder at himself that he hadn't thought of it initially.

There's a reason you didn't.

He ignored the thought and smiled. Then turned to St George, who was still holding his tumbler of brandy and staring at them, his expression impassive.

'My plans have changed,' Enzo said shortly, looking the other man straight in the eye. 'I'll take my son. And I'll take your wife as well.'

Silence crashed over the room, heavy and final.

Matilda didn't think it was possible to be any more shocked than she already had been, but apparently it was very possible. Very possible indeed.

Enzo was going to *take her*? What on earth did he mean by that?

You know what you want him to mean.

Her breathing quickened and despite herself all she could think about was that moment in the hallway, when he'd had his hands on either side of her head, his golden eyes pinning her like a butterfly on a board. And his body had been inches away, the heat of it burning through all that expensive wool. His beautiful mouth had been right there and she thought he might have kissed her. And part of her had been afraid that he would while another part had wanted it desperately.

But he hadn't. And thank God. She didn't want to go there again and most certainly not with him.

Because you know what will happen when you do.

No. Nothing would happen. She was stronger than that now.

Henry's white eyebrows had risen into his hairline. 'I think you'll find my wife might have other ideas,' he said mildly.

But Matilda remained silent, shock still pulsing through her.

It had taken her a couple of moments to get herself together in the hallway upstairs, and then a couple more for it to filter through that Enzo probably hadn't left to re-join the party as if nothing had happened.

He'd probably gone to arrange the kidnap of her son, which meant that she had no time to sag against the wall trying not to have a breakdown.

So she'd sprung into action, rushing off to see where he'd got to, tracking him down—much to her horror—to Henry's study.

That he'd told Henry he was Simon's father was bad enough, but the fact that he'd also told Henry he was going to take Simon away was even worse.

Simon loved Henry. He knew Henry wasn't his father—Matilda had made sure of that—but he and Henry had forged a relationship all the same, and for him to be taken away not only from her but from Henry as well…

It made her throat tighten. Made her chest feel as though someone had ripped her heart straight from it.

She'd lost her parents when she'd been a child and she knew all too well what it felt like to lose the only people in the world who wanted you. Who loved you. And, even though she and Henry wouldn't actually be dead, they still wouldn't be there.

She couldn't bear the thought of not being there for Simon.

Which meant she couldn't let that happen, and if that involved doing battle with Enzo Cardinali then she'd have to do battle. Rocking the boat and making a fuss went against everything she'd been brought up to believe, but she'd do it for her son.

Except that Enzo clearly had other ideas.

'What do you mean you'll "take" me?' she asked, her voice sounding strange and shrill in the silence of the room.

Enzo turned his head, blazing amber pinning her to the spot. 'I mean, you're correct. I can't take the child away from everything that is familiar to him. I will have to take something familiar to him with

me instead.' Something shifted in his gaze, something that made her throat close and a perverse kind
of excitement tighten inside her. 'That's you, in case
you were wondering.'

Her mouth had gone as dry as the Sahara. 'You're
insane.'

'No. What I am is ruthless. I've had too many
things taken from me, *cara*, and I am done with it.
What's mine stays mine, and that includes Simon.'

'Matilda is not yours to take, though.' Henry's
tone was still mild.

Enzo whipped round to face him. 'What? You
think I want her as a lover? That I would touch another man's wife?' He made it sound as if he'd never
heard of anything so ridiculous. 'I think not. No,
all I require is a month or two of her presence, just
enough to settle Simon in his new home.'

A burst of anger pierced Matilda's shock. The
sheer, damn arrogance of him. Talking about her as
if she wasn't there, as if she was a piece of property
he could keep or dispose of as he wished.

And, more than anything else, the assumption
that her presence wouldn't be required after Simon
had 'settled in'.

'I am his mother,' she said icily. 'And I will be
his mother for ever. A month or two of my presence
will not be enough.'

Enzo turned again, his attention focused on her
once more. 'Then stay. I have no objections. The only
requirement I have is that Simon lives with me. You
can come and go as you please.'

She took an unsteady breath. 'So you're basically saying I have to uproot my life in England and move to…wherever you are. Just like that.'

'Why not? You decided not to tell me I had a son. Just like that.'

'You make it sound as if it that was an easy decision.'

'And wasn't it? As easy as simply deciding not to pick up that phone and make a second call.'

Emotion choked her, shame, regret and a whole lot of other things all tangling and knotting inside her.

So many mistakes. So many things she had to make up for. But why should her child suffer for everything she'd done wrong? And why should Henry suffer too?

She shot her husband a glance. He'd poured himself another large glass of brandy and met her gaze with a certain sympathy. 'You should have told me, Mattie,' he said quietly. 'Especially considering I invited him here.'

The sense of shame grew larger. Yes, she knew she should have. But she hadn't. She'd thought she could avoid the situation entirely.

Stupid. She'd been stupid.

Her eyes pricked with tears, but she swallowed them back.

No, she wouldn't cry, and certainly not while Enzo was staring at her, judging her.

'I'm sorry, Henry.' She tried to ignore the man standing in front of her, though that was impossible with the room so full of his restless intensity. 'I know I should have. I just…' She stopped.

Henry was too understanding. Too kind. She didn't deserve him and she knew it.

'Well?' Enzo demanded, ignoring Henry, his gaze on her as if she was the only other thing in the universe. 'What's it to be? Will you come with me to Milan tomorrow or not?'

She tried a last-ditch protest. 'If you take Simon, I'll call the police.'

'No, you won't.' It was Henry, sounding tired.

Matilda blinked, staring at her husband, conscious of Enzo's gaze on her. 'What do you mean, no?'

'You think Cardinali here will go without a fight?' Henry gestured at Enzo with his brandy glass. 'He won't and you know it.'

'Then I'll fight back,' she insisted, not quite sure why Henry would give in like that.

'Try, *cara*,' Enzo murmured, his voice low enough that only she heard it, and full of sensual threat. 'See how far you get.'

'Think of the scandal.' Henry shook his head. 'It'll be all over the gossip sites, all over the web within hours. I don't want that and I certainly don't want that for Simon. Do you?'

No. She didn't. And it made sense. The news that Henry St George's child wasn't actually his and was, in fact, the child of billionaire property developer Enzo Cardinali would keep the scandal sheets going for months.

And they wouldn't only be all over her like flies

on spilled food, they'd be all over Simon as well. He would be starting school in a year. People's memories were short, but the Internet was for ever.

'No,' she said thickly, feeling her control of the situation start to slip from her fingers. 'I don't want that.'

'They'll find out eventually,' Henry murmured, 'But at least let Simon have a couple of weeks without the paparazzi in his face.'

He was right. Of course he was right. Yet...

They'd never been a true husband and wife, only good friends. And they'd had a good few years together. But he wasn't even arguing with Enzo. He seemed prepared simply to let her go. Both her *and* Simon. Without even a protest.

Did he even care? Did they even matter to him?

'Well, I'll leave you two to sort it out between yourselves.' Henry put his brandy glass down and moved towards the door as if everything had been decided already. 'Try not to destroy my study in the process.' The door shut behind him, the sound of the click echoing inside Matilda like the sound of a tomb closing.

The silence in the room was deafening.

Enzo was standing near the fireplace. He hadn't moved, but the intentness of his focus made her feel as though all the air had been sucked out of the room.

She didn't want to meet his relentless golden stare. Didn't want to know what he thought of her husband surrendering her without a single protest.

It was humiliating.

'And so,' he said at last, softly. 'Your decision has been made for you, I think.'

So you made a mistake. Deal with it. This is for Simon, remember?

Yes, it was. And, if there was one thing she'd come to realise about a man like Enzo Cardinali, it was that like all predators he'd exploit any weakness he could find in order to get a kill. Which meant that if she was going to survive this she couldn't give him any.

She had to armour herself and armour herself well.

Matilda steeled her spine, lifted her head and looked at him.

There was triumph in his gaze, which she'd expected. But also something else that she hadn't. A heat that had burned her to ashes back on the island. The same heat that had nearly incinerated her where she'd stood in the hallway.

Not just you, remember? He burned too.

No, she hadn't forgotten. Not about the power that had been hers in the hot, scented night. A power that might still be hers, if she had the courage to wield it.

'Don't get ahead of yourself,' she said, holding his gaze. 'I haven't said yes yet.'

He smiled, a hungry, dark kind of smile, as if he knew something she didn't. 'But you will, *cara*. Most certainly you will. Now, you should go pack for yourself and Simon. We'll leave for Milan first thing in the morning.'

CHAPTER FOUR

ENZO SAT IN the comfort of his private jet and regarded the small boy sitting opposite him, who was watching him in turn with equal seriousness.

The child's black hair was spiked up, his Cardinali golden eyes large. He had his mother's freckles sprinkled across his nose, and her chin too, angled right now with the same determination.

A fine-looking boy. But that was no surprise; he had the Cardinali royal genes.

You'd better hope he has none of the royal flaws.

Enzo ignored the thought, aware of Matilda sitting beside her son, pale and silent. She hadn't said a word to Enzo the entire morning.

He didn't like it. It reminded him too much of his mother's pointed silences. Then again, pressing would make it look as if he cared and he didn't. No, this wouldn't be easy for her, but then spending four whole years not knowing he had a son wasn't easy for him either.

'I don't like you,' his son said with finality after a moment.

Matilda stiffened. 'Simon, don't say—'

'It's fine.' Enzo wasn't bothered. He didn't expect instant love from the boy, especially given he was a complete stranger to him. 'You don't have to like me,' he went on, addressing the child. 'But I'm still your father.'

Simon had taken in his stride the news that his father had turned up out of the blue and was intent on taking him and his mother to Italy. As long as there was a swimming pool, he'd said, he didn't mind.

The boy frowned and for a second Enzo saw his own father in him, which wasn't a comfortable thought. 'Why didn't you come before?'

Enzo didn't have to ask what Simon meant and for a second he caught Matilda's grey stare. Colour flushed her cheekbones, a pretty stain of pink.

She was lovely this morning, even in another jeans and T-shirt outfit, with her hair pulled back from her face, the rest of it tumbling over her shoulders in a riot of red.

Desire shifted inside him, lean and hungry as a starving leopard, but he ignored it the way he ignored the anger that shifted along with it.

He would never let himself be at the mercy of his emotions or his baser desires. Not again.

'I didn't come before because I didn't know I had a son,' he said, because why should he spare her feelings when she hadn't spared his? 'Not until your mother told me last night.'

The boy's frown deepened. 'And will you be my father for ever?'

'Yes,' he said, meeting his son's gaze. 'I will be your father for ever.'

Simon chewed his bottom lip. 'Okay. But I already have a daddy. I can't call you Daddy too.'

Enzo's anger twisted, though it wasn't directed at his son. Because, of course, the boy was presumably talking about St George, which was understandable, given that St George was the only father figure he'd ever known.

Enzo didn't look at Matilda, though he could feel the distress radiating from her. He didn't feel sorry for her, not one single iota.

She was the one who'd created this situation. She could deal with it.

'Of course not,' Enzo agreed. 'You're part Italian. You will call me Papa.'

'Papa,' the boy echoed, copying Enzo's accent. Then he shrugged as if he had no feeling about it one way or the other. 'Can I play on your phone, Mummy?'

Enzo reached for his own phone before realising belatedly that the child probably wouldn't want it since there were no games on it.

But Matilda had already taken hers out and had given it to her son, who took it happily. 'Go and sit over there, Simon,' she murmured, indicating a long, low couch on the other side of the cabin. 'I need to talk to Mr Cardinali.'

'I think you mean "Papa",' Enzo corrected, because he did not want her forgetting, not for one second, who the boy's father was.

Something flashed in Matilda's eyes, but she didn't say anything, shooing the boy away to the couch where he could play his games in peace.

Once the child had settled, she said, 'I think it's time you told me what the plan is.'

Enzo sat back in his seat, staring at her. Oh, yes, she was certainly beautiful today. Her T-shirt was grey, deepening the storm-cloud colour of her eyes. She wore no make-up and when she'd met him in the car that morning, although she'd brought plenty of luggage for Simon she'd brought only a small bag with her.

Obviously she was driving home the point that she wasn't making an effort for him, nor was she intending to stay very long.

Unfortunately for her, he was going to ensure that she stayed as long as Simon needed her to, regardless of how she felt about it. Because when he'd said he would take her last night, he'd meant it.

He wouldn't leave his son without something familiar. And she was that something familiar. At least, until the boy had got to know him, naturally enough.

The satisfaction of the night before returned, settling the coal of anger that smouldered inside him. Yes, taking the boy and Matilda too had been the right decision. The *only* decision.

He'd met with St George that morning before they'd left and had made an offer on Isola Sacra, doubling his previous offer, because he didn't want to mess around now he had his son. St George had taken it without argument, the same way he'd accepted Enzo's insistence on Matilda coming with him the night before.

It had puzzled Enzo a little that the man had made no protest, especially considering that he and St George's wife had once been lovers. Enzo himself wouldn't have been so accepting if the positions had been reversed, after all. But he hadn't thought about it in any depth at the time, too pleased with how everything had turned out with so little fuss.

However, reflecting on it now, St George's lack of protest was…odd.

'Plan?' Enzo murmured, studying her. 'What plan?'

Her lovely mouth tightened. 'You know what I'm talking about. You haven't told me a thing about what's going to happen when we get to Milan.'

'I haven't told you anything because you haven't asked.'

The colour in her cheeks intensified, anger glittering in her eyes.

Well, *that* was better than silence. Oh, yes, a lot better. Strong women had always appealed to him, which made it a great pity that she was someone else's. Because, now that he thought about it, he wouldn't mind revisiting a few old memories. It was only sex. And perhaps *he* would be the one to leave her with nothing but an empty bed and cold sheets.

'Well,' Matilda said tightly, folding her hands in her lap. 'Now I'm asking.'

'What will happen?' he echoed. 'Simon will stay in my villa until Isola Sacra, the island I've just purchased from your husband, is ready for guests. And then I will take him there.'

She blinked, her lashes glinting red in the sun coming through the plane's windows. He remembered that rusty colour, the same glint as when she'd lain back on the blanket he'd put down on the sand and looked up at him, smiling as she'd idly stroked his bare shoulder...

'Island?' Matilda's voice was sharp. 'What island?'

Enzo controlled the heat that curled through him at the memory, ignoring the small tug of something that felt uncomfortably like pain. 'The island your husband refused to sell to me unless I attended his ridiculous house party.' He kept his voice cold. 'Luckily, whatever scruples he had about selling it were easily dispensed with when I doubled the price.'

She looked away, as if something about his statement had bothered her. 'And what about me?'

'What about you?' He couldn't quite drag his gaze away from her profile, fixating on the shape of her mouth. It was full, the bottom lip sulky. He remembered biting on that bottom lip and making her shiver.

She didn't appear to notice his stare, too busy gazing out of the window. 'Presumably you want me to stay with Simon?'

'Of course I want you to stay with Simon. That's the whole reason you're here, after all.' He also wanted to reach out, take her chin in his fingers and tilt her head back so he could look into her stormy grey eyes. See what she was thinking, though why he wanted to do that he had no idea.

Very suddenly, she turned her head and her gaze met his head-on, and the challenge glowing deep in it hit him like a punch to the gut. 'Simon and I can find our own accommodation,' she said, as if she were throwing down a gauntlet. 'We don't need to stay with you.'

He went still as the hot coal in his gut flared into life.

Dio, did she really think that challenging him about this was a good idea? Now? After what she'd done to him? And not only him, but her son too. Because, yes, in depriving Enzo of Simon she'd also deprived Simon of Enzo.

A boy needed his father.

Pity yours was never there for you when you needed him.

The small flame of anger burned higher. No, of course his father hadn't been there for Enzo. He'd been too full of rage and blame at the change of their circumstances, shouting and railing at his wife. Shouting and railing at Enzo and Dante too. It had been like water off a duck's back for Dante, but not for Enzo. He was the oldest son. He was the heir. He was responsible.

Quite literally.

A shiver of ice snaked down his spine but he shoved the thought from his head before it could form.

His father had been a terror after he'd lost his

throne, and after his wife had left him he'd been even worse. He'd simply pretended Enzo didn't exist.

But you deserved that.

Yes, well, maybe he had. He and his father deserved each other, at least that was what his mother had flung at him after she'd discovered he'd emptied down the sink all the bottles of wine she'd had stashed away. He'd only been trying to help her, but she hadn't seen it that way.

'How dare you?' she'd shouted at him. *'So selfish and judgmental and controlling. Just like your father.'*

Whatever… Right now, Simon didn't deserve it, and Simon was what mattered. He would make sure he'd never treat his son the way his father had treated him. Or his mother, for that matter.

'No,' Enzo said with finality. 'He will not be staying anywhere but with me. And so will you.'

Anger glittered in her eyes, like small shards of lightning. 'Have you really thought about what having a child around is like? Four-year-olds aren't exactly quiet. They have no concept of—'

'I don't care. You both will remain with me and that is final.'

Her chin adopted a mutinous slant and he found himself almost hoping she would push him further, harder, so he could…

So you can what?

Enzo shifted in his seat, annoyed with himself. He was letting her get under his skin, which was stupid in the extreme. Four years ago he'd let her do more than that; he'd let her almost find her way to his soul and he would never allow that to happen again. Most especially given that she was someone else's.

Except that anger in her eyes fascinated him, challenged him. Demanded a response from him. A response he wanted to give.

Perhaps he would have to find another woman in Milan. It didn't have to be her.

Matilda looked away again out of the window of the plane. 'How long are you expecting to have him in Italy?'

Enzo had thought of this. He'd spent all night thinking about it. 'Four years. You had him in England for four, he can spend four with me in Italy. After that, well, I'm a reasonable man. We can discuss more formal custody arrangements.'

She glanced back at him sharply. 'Four years?' The colour in her cheeks ebbed, her dusting of freckles stark against her pale skin.

'Of course four years.' He stared back, letting her see how serious he was. 'You really think I'd want him for a week or two, only to send him back like an unwanted gift?'

'But…he doesn't speak any Italian. And he's never lived anywhere else. And he doesn't know anyone. England is his home.'

'No,' Enzo said. 'Italy will be his home. Isola Sacra will be his home.'

An expression that looked like anguish crossed her face. 'But…he's just a little boy, Enzo. He doesn't know he's not coming back. He didn't have a chance to say goodbye to anything.'

Neither did you.

Enzo ignored the thought, hardening himself. 'Yes, and it's easier when they're young. He won't remember.'

'You did,' Matilda said, her eyes glittering.

And there it was, the reminder again. Of what he'd told her, everything about himself that he'd laid bare. The pain of losing his home, of losing his history, of losing his roots. A glimpse of his soul.

Dio, he should never have told her.

'I was fifteen.' He ignored the past she'd been stupid enough to bring up. 'Simon is four. He won't remember. My brother didn't.' That Dante had been eleven and Enzo knew full well he actually had remembered was beside the point.

Simon *was* young. And if Enzo did his job properly his son wouldn't even remember he'd been English in the first place.

Matilda held his gaze for a second and he could see the anger blazing in it, the fire at the heart of her burning high and hot in defence of her child.

He approved. His own mother hadn't fought for him; she'd simply left.

Maybe she'd been right to leave.

Perhaps she had been. Again, though, beside the point. The fact was that if Matilda thought that getting angry would force him to do what she wanted she was mistaken.

Her lashes lowered all of a sudden, gazing down

at her hands clasped tightly in her lap. Her fingers were long, delicate, and he remembered what they'd felt like on his body. Wrapped around his shaft…

'I'm sorry, Enzo.' Her voice sounded scraped raw. 'I know you're angry. I made a mistake. I'm not sure what else I can do.'

There was a note in the words that hooked into a part of him he thought he'd buried after he'd returned to Italy from the island. A part he didn't want to acknowledge.

He ignored it, hardening himself even further.

'There is nothing you can do,' he said. 'Except give me everything I want.'

Matilda fought the anger that smouldered inside her like a hot coal. She wanted to get up and scream in his face that it was okay to punish her, but how could he take his anger at her out on their son? Because, no matter what he thought, that was exactly what he was doing.

But she stayed silent. Things were already as bad as they could get. She didn't want to make them any worse.

It's your own fault. You should have told him. You shouldn't have let fear get in the way.

As if she didn't know that already.

She took a deep breath, attempting to calm herself, but the scent of his aftershave surrounded her, rich and spicy, and all she could think about was how delicious he smelled.

God, she did *not* want to think about that.

Getting Simon up that morning and ready to leave had been a small nightmare in itself, especially when she hadn't slept for more than an hour the previous night.

Henry had been distant saying goodbye to Simon—understandably—and even more so when he'd said goodbye to her. He hadn't offered her any reassuring words or even a hug. He'd simply nodded and told her he'd see her later.

It had felt as if he was saying goodbye for good.

An old and familiar pain laced through her anger. His apparent lack of interest had made her feel like she was ten years old again, an orphan thrust on her uncle and aunt who'd been too busy dealing with their own grief and shock to spare much in the way of comfort for her.

They'd taken her without protest but she knew deep down that they'd never wanted kids. And they really hadn't wanted her.

No one does.

Matilda's jaw tightened. She shoved the thought away. No, giving in to her anger at Enzo and letting the past he brought trailing in his wake get to her was not what she was going to do. That wasn't what was best for Simon and that was what she had to concentrate on now.

Her son was the most important thing in her life. And, yes, she'd made a mistake in not contacting Enzo about him, but she couldn't keep focusing on that. She had to move on.

She didn't want to look at the man lounging in

the lush comfort of the private jet's leather seats, all lean, muscular physicality and electric presence.

He was in another of his exquisitely tailored suits—dark-blue this time, the contrast making his eyes look even more golden than they already were—the cut drawing attention to his wide, powerful shoulders, lean hips and long legs. He had one ankle resting on the opposite knee, leaning back in the seat, his elbow on the arm rest, his chin in his palm. He watched her with all the focus of a bird of prey, all unblinking golden eyes and an unmistakable hunger.

He wants you, no matter how cold he sounds.

Matilda kept her gaze on her hands. She'd thought he wanted her last night. Was it still true?

The anger inside her became shivery, excited almost. Which only made her angrier. She didn't want to feel this way about him. Didn't want to remember those nights she'd spent with him. Didn't want to be so painfully, physically aware of him.

You can use that if need be, remember?

'So,' Enzo said when she didn't break the silence. 'Tell me everything there is to know about my son. And when I say everything, *cara*, I do mean *everything*.'

She ignored the voice in her head. Shoved away the unwelcome pull of physical desire.

'Okay.' She steeled herself, lifting her gaze to his. 'Where shall I start?'

His amber eyes burned. God, how could she have forgotten how fierce he could be? This merciless, uncompromising man might not be the Enzo Cardinali that she'd met and nearly fallen for but the ferocity she remembered was still there—or at least a colder, harder version of it.

'Where else should you start but at the beginning? From the moment you realised you were pregnant and decided not to tell me.'

So, he wasn't going to let her forget it nor was he going to forgive her for it. Well, he'd already told her he wouldn't, and he was apparently a man of his word.

She'd simply have to deal with it.

'Okay,' she said and began.

He hadn't been kidding when he'd said he wanted to know everything. He had questions about every aspect of Simon's life, from what kind of food he'd liked as a baby to what kind of toys he'd preferred as a toddler. Enzo wanted to know all about Simon's milestones, whether he had friends and how well he slept. What kinds of things he liked to do and whether he'd had any illnesses. Enzo's interest was so focused and intent that she found herself almost relaxing as she told him about Simon's life, because she was as interested in talking about her son as Enzo was interested in hearing about him.

'And did you work?' Enzo asked eventually. 'Was he in day care?'

'No.' Resolutely she didn't think about the degree she'd had to put on hold. 'Simon was my sole focus.'

He gave no sign of whether he approved of this or not, his handsome face expressionless. 'But you wanted to go to university. I remember you telling me.'

The words gave her a brief electric shock. He'd remembered that? She'd remembered everything that he'd told her, but she hadn't thought he'd remember what she'd said to him. The hopes and dreams she'd revealed that first night, caught up in the intensity of his touch and the sheer wonder that someone like him would want her.

She fought to keep the shock from her face. 'I decided to put that on hold. Simon was more important.'

'But you could have gone. Your husband surely would have been able to afford a nanny or day care.'

Henry had indeed offered, but she'd refused. Her son came first and always had done. 'It was better for Simon to be my sole focus,' she said stiffly.

Enzo's gaze was sharp and she had the uncomfortable feeling that he was seeing things in her she didn't understand herself. 'You wanted to go. That was your dream, you said.'

'Yes, and I didn't. What does it matter what I did or didn't do, anyway? You wanted to know about Simon, not me.'

'And you are his mother. You have an effect on him.'

'I was fine with the decision.' She could feel her hands clasping each other more tightly at the faint hollow echo in her voice, as if she didn't believe it herself. 'University could wait. Simon was only going to be little once.'

The words fell into the space between them, heavy as lead.

Enzo's expression tightened at the reminder of all he'd missed out on.

Oh, God, why had she said that? Then again, there was nothing about this situation that wouldn't be hurtful. There were sharp edges everywhere and neither of them was exempt from the pain of those cuts.

He shifted in his seat, the fabric of his suit trousers tightening over his thighs. 'St George didn't seem to be too upset at losing his wife. He didn't even give you a goodbye kiss.'

The observation hurt, and she was under no illusions; somehow Enzo knew that. He was hell-bent on punishing her, apparently.

'No,' she said levelly, swallowing back the pain, determined not to show him that he was getting to her. 'Henry is very old school. He doesn't do public displays of affection.'

'How strange then that he married you so soon after you returned to England. Four months, wasn't it? Or was it more that you had to hide the fact that you were pregnant with my child?'

He didn't know that she'd been promised to Henry. That was the one thing she hadn't told him. As far as he knew, she'd been single, taking some time out for a holiday before she went home and started university.

She was powerless against the flush that she could feel creeping up her neck and heating her cheeks.

'Like I told you, Henry knew from the beginning that Simon wasn't his.'

'He must have been very much in love with you to marry you anyway.'

She could tell Enzo the truth right now. Tell him that her marriage was in name only and that Henry had never been a husband to her, only a friend. But there was a small, stubborn part of her that didn't want to. Her marriage had nothing whatsoever to do with him. She might owe him the truth when it came to Simon, but not when it came to her reasons for marrying Henry.

He'd told her on their last night on the island, when they'd shared their hopes for the future, that he wanted to reclaim his lost kingdom. Oh, he knew he could never go back to what he'd once had, but he could recreate a home somewhere else. A home that included a wife and children. A family.

He'd even told her what his ideal wife would be like: strong and passionate. Brave. Beautiful. A woman who knew her own mind. A woman who was his equal, a queen to his king.

Not her, in other words.

She'd told herself it was just as well, since she'd already committed to marrying Henry, but those words had stuck inside her like a thorn, settling deep inside her heart. And she'd never managed to get them out.

Of course she wasn't any of those things. She'd never been any of those things and never would be. She was simply the orphan that nobody wanted, who'd been passed on from her aunt and uncle to Henry as easily as Henry had passed her on to Enzo in turn.

But then, Enzo didn't know that, did he?

'Yes.' She held his gaze with sudden ferocity, daring him to contradict her. 'Henry was desperately in love with me. He couldn't wait to marry me.'

Enzo's gaze flared, bright, brilliant and hot. 'And did he bed you just as desperately?'

The words sent a bolt of electricity shooting down her spine. 'That's none of your business.' She managed to keep her voice cold. 'In fact, my entire marriage is none of your business. This is about Simon, not me.'

Enzo didn't move, his posture radiating a kind of leashed tension that made the very air between them vibrate.

Her muscles tightened, her skin prickling all over.

She wanted to breathe but couldn't. As if taking a breath would make something snap, or break something that couldn't be repaired.

A muscle flicked in his jaw then abruptly he reached down and pulled out his phone from his pocket, looking down at the screen as if the moment of electric tension between had never existed. 'I need to prepare for Simon's arrival. Tell me everything he might need.'

Her heart raced, awareness of him prickling all over her skin, restlessness coiling inside her.

She dug her nails into her palms, gritting her teeth. She didn't want to tell him anything more.

She didn't want to tell him anything at all. But that wouldn't be fair on Simon, so she gave him the information he wanted.

He didn't say a word, merely nodded then pushed himself out of his seat, pacing down the length of the cabin as he began issuing orders into his phone in rapid Italian.

Matilda tried to drag her gaze from him, tried to concentrate on thinking about what the hell she was going to do next, because she had no idea. But it was next to impossible with Enzo pacing up and down, filling the cabin with his intense, electric presence.

It made the rest of the journey to Milan almost intolerable.

Enzo didn't sit down for the remainder of the trip and didn't speak to her again. Instead he kept pacing while he talked into his phone, and it didn't matter how much Matilda tried to block him out, her brain seemed intent on concentrating on him and the rise and fall of his deep, cold voice to the exclusion of everything else.

By the end of the flight she felt like she'd been through the wringer.

Simon, on the other hand, was a ball of electric excitement.

After the jet touched down and they were disembarking, he showed no sign of his apparent dislike of Enzo, keeping up a running commentary and peppering him with questions as one of Enzo's staff showed them to the car that waited for them and their luggage was loaded.

Matilda tried to quiet him, not wanting him to keep bothering his father, but Enzo shook his head. 'Let him talk,' he said. 'He can ask me anything.' Then he proceeded to give his son all his attention, not at all bothered by the boy's constant questions.

Matilda sat back in the seat as the long, sleek black car moved through the dense Milan traffic, a strange sensation sitting inside her.

Enzo was pointing at something out of the window, Simon kneeling on the seat and peering out, asking yet more questions. He hadn't looked at her once since getting off the plane, all his attention totally taken up by Enzo.

Even Henry didn't get quite this much attention. Then again, Henry hadn't shown quite as much interest in him as Enzo had.

Certainly it made her feel almost…superfluous.

What if Enzo was right? What if Simon didn't miss England? What if he didn't miss Henry? What if he settled into life in Italy as though he'd born here? What if he never wanted to go home?

And, if he doesn't, what are you going to do?

Cold seeped through her.

Four years, Enzo had said. Four years he was going to keep her son. And where did that leave her? She could fight him, could drag this to the courts, drag her son through the media circus that would no doubt ensue. But she'd get no support from Henry— he'd already made that clear—which meant that if she did she'd have to pay her own legal fees. An impossibility considering that her money all came from Henry anyway.

Which left her only options either staying in Italy to be near her son or going back to England and home, her contact with Simon reduced to visiting whenever she could.

God, she hated the thought of both options. If she stayed in Italy, she'd be a stranger here. She knew no one except Enzo, didn't speak the language and wasn't qualified to get any kind of job. She'd be here without support, alone.

Her throat closed.

Unwanted by anyone yet again...

No. What a pathetic thing to think. Her son might be caught up with his father right now, but *he* wanted her. And, if she had to stay here to be with him and bear being a bit lonely for four years, then she would.

She would do what she had to for him.

And what about Henry?

Another thing to think about. Would he be upset if she chose to stay in Italy with Simon? After all, the whole basis for their marriage was that she would be his companion. Would he mind if she only visited him? Would he demand the return of the money he'd paid to her aunt and uncle after he'd married her?

That wouldn't be Henry's style. Then again, she hadn't thought he'd let her go without even a protest when Enzo had demanded her presence in Italy, so what did she know?

Simon was chattering on about something, point-ing as he did so, completely absorbed in the sights outside the window. Enzo responded calmly, his hand resting on the seat next to his son, his body angled protectively at the boy's back despite the seatbelt.

Enzo had only known of Simon's existence for less than twelve hours and already he was acting like a father.

Henry had been good to Simon, of that there was no doubt, but in four years he'd never acted particu-larly fatherly.

'He needs his father,' Enzo had told her.

Tears pricked unexpectedly behind her eyes and she had to blink hard to get rid of them. Of course Simon needed him. That was why she was here, so her son could get to know him. So Simon could have *both* his parents.

She knew what it was like to have neither, so how could she even contemplate leaving him and going back to Henry? There *was* no other option for her. She would have to stay.

The certainty of it settled down inside her as the car moved through the traffic, leaving the city.

Wait…leaving the city?

She frowned. 'I thought you lived in Milan?'

'I do. I have several properties there. But you and Simon will be going to my villa just outside the city.' He looked at his son. 'It has a private park with woods you can play in.'

The little boy's eyes lit up. 'And a pool?'

'Yes. There is a pool.'

Finally Simon deigned to look at her. 'Mummy! There's a pool! Can I go swimming?'

A private park. With woods. And a swimming pool. She wasn't going to be able to compete with that, was she? Even Henry's home in England didn't have a swimming pool.

'Of course.' She made herself smile. 'Good thing I put in your swimsuit, isn't it?'

But Simon was already asking Enzo more about the woods and whether there would be a horse there. Or even a dog, because he liked dogs, and could he have a puppy?

A heavy feeling settled down on her, one that didn't lift even when half an hour later the iron gates that guarded Enzo's estate opened and the car drove through a stately avenue of trees, pulling up outside an historic Italian villa of pale honey-coloured stone.

The grounds were beautiful, the house even more so, decorated along luxurious yet uncluttered lines with nods to the past in the art on the walls and the antique furniture that graced the rooms. There were plenty of modern touches here and there too, such as a state-of-the-art home entertainment system, including security, central heating and Internet streaming.

Simon loved the room that Enzo had given him, with a curtained bed and a big toy box in the middle. There were views out over the woods at the back of the villa and glimpses of the promised pool. But what made Matilda's throat feel tight all over again were the small personal items that Enzo had somehow managed to fly from Henry's house in England and get here in time for their arrival. A stuffed giraffe that Simon had accidentally left behind and his favourite Lego spaceship. The giraffe was on the blue curtained bed, while the spaceship took pride of place on a dresser.

Simon shrieked with delight and launched himself at his giraffe, while Enzo strolled into the room behind him, his eyes full of the same fierce satisfaction that had burned in them all day.

'Signora St George?' It was Maria, the housekeeper who'd greeted them as they'd arrived.

Matilda turned.

'Come this way,' Maria said. 'I will show you to your room.'

She didn't want to go. She wanted to stay with her son, make sure he was okay. Make sure he didn't forget her in the excitement of being in this new place with his father.

But she let herself be led away, Simon's excited voice fading as she was led down various cool tiled hallways with luxurious silk runners on the floor and art in ornate frames on the whitewashed walls. Tall windows let in the buttery late-summer light, giving everything a warm glow.

Would Enzo want her living here? Or would she have to find a place nearby? He'd said he had no objections to her living in his house with Simon, but… would she want to?

It'll be no different than it was living with Henry. What's the problem with that?

She didn't know. Because, yes, that was exactly what she'd been doing the past four years. There wouldn't be anything different about living here except the country and the language.

The room the housekeeper showed her to was beautiful.

Pale blue walls and an antique four-poster bed hung with thick white curtains. Beneath one tall window was a couch upholstered in white linen, with lots of silk cushions scattered on it in many shades of blue.

There was no sign of the single bag she'd brought with her that had been whisked away as soon as she'd got out of the car, but a closer investigation of the drawers in a beautiful oak dresser soon revealed that the meagre lot of clothes she'd brought with her had been folded and put away.

Along with a whole lot of other clothes that she hadn't brought with her. Expensive clothes. In what looked like her size.

An uncomfortable feeling gathered inside her.

She went into the beautiful, white-tiled *en suite* bathroom to discover that, not only had her toiletries been put away, they'd also been added to: expensive bath products and skin care, along with a few other feminine things.

She went back out into the bedroom again and stood there, the uncomfortable feeling growing bigger and heavier inside her, and she wasn't sure why.

It was Enzo, obviously, who'd bought all that stuff. For her.

Slowly, she sat down on the embroidered white quilt that was spread over the bed, the uncomfortable feeling becoming oddly painful.

A memory sat in her head, of being shown to her room at her aunt and uncle's house. There had been nothing of hers in there, nothing except what she'd brought in her suitcase. Her aunt and uncle hadn't bought her anything special or made any effort to make the room feel less like a guest room. They hadn't noticed that she'd been growing and that she'd needed new clothes. Not noticed like a mother would notice. She'd had to tell them that her jeans were too short and that her T-shirts were too tight.

But here, now, Enzo had bought her clothes. And toiletries. There were none of the personal things that he'd brought for Simon, but still. He'd thought about it. He'd thought about her. And, more, he was clearly expecting her to be staying *here*. In this villa. With him and her son.

She didn't know how she felt about that.

'Do you have everything you need?'

Enzo's deep, cold voice was like a slap of icy water against her skin, making her jump.

She looked up sharply to find him in the doorway of the bedroom, leaning one shoulder against the frame. His arms were folded across his broad chest, his gaze sharp, the expression on his beautiful face impenetrable.

'Yes.' She rose from the bed. 'I thought I'd brought

everything I needed with me, but apparently I hadn't. There seems to be a lot of additional clothing in the drawers.'

'It's for you.' He tilted his head, staring at her like an eagle staring at a rabbit. 'You wanted to stay here with Simon, which means you'll be here a while.'

'Four years, or so I hear.'

He lifted a shoulder casually, as if he didn't care one way or another. 'That's up to you.'

A small devil needled at her, wanting to disturb his apparent disinterest. 'My husband might have something to say about that.'

'Really?' One black brow rose. 'Didn't seem like it.'

She flushed, humiliation sweeping through her the way it had when he'd mentioned Henry's lack of response on the jet. She tried not to let him see it. 'You seem quite fascinated with my marriage. What's up with that?'

'Purely academic. Your relationship with St George will obviously have had an effect on my son.'

'Henry has been nothing but good—'

'And I don't dispute that,' Enzo interrupted. 'But how has St George treated you?'

She blinked. 'What do you mean? What's that got to do with anything?'

'A strong, loving marriage has an effect on children, as has a cold, distant one. Or a violent one.' The words were casual but the look in his eyes was anything but. 'I want to know what kind of marriage yours is.'

Give him what he wants otherwise he'll never stop asking.

It was true. Easier by far simply to tell him and then he'd never have to ask her again.

Except then she'd have to confess to the reality of her marriage with Henry. How she'd done it for her aunt and uncle. For money. How she'd been bought and paid for because he'd wanted a companion rather than a wife. How he'd told her he was fond of her, only to let her go the moment Enzo had snapped his fingers and threatened a scandal...

'It is a loving marriage.' The lie came so easily. 'Henry was desperately in love with me and I was with him. Simon has been treated as a son.'

Something sharp and hot glittered in the depths of Enzo's eyes. 'He didn't protest when I told him I would take you with me. He didn't even kiss you goodbye.'

Matilda lifted her chin. 'Henry is a very private man. I told you, public displays of affection aren't his style. And what was the point in protesting? He knows I'll come back to him.'

'And how exactly is that going to work? With your son here?'

Anger was growing inside her at his questions and the harsh note of condemnation in his voice. Yes, she'd made a mistake with Enzo. But marrying Henry and the past four years spent creating a happy home for her son was not one. 'I'll figure it out,' she said just as coldly. 'It won't affect you and it won't affect Simon.'

'But it will affect both me and Simon if you're going off every weekend to bed your husband.'

'Why?' she said before she could stop herself. 'Are you jealous? It's been four years, Enzo, come on.'

CHAPTER FIVE

MATILDA STOOD IN the middle of the room with her hands clasped in front of her, the curls falling down around her shoulders the colour of fire and passion, yet her grey eyes remained cool as mountain mist.

Finally, she was here. In his house. In the room he'd set aside for her.

And now she was talking about her husband, how in love with him she was and how in love St George was with her.

It shouldn't have mattered to him and yet he couldn't deny the furious, almost territorial anger that coiled and twisted inside him like a cut snake.

He didn't understand it. What did he care that she loved her husband? As far as he was concerned love didn't exist anyway since he'd certainly seen no evidence of it. And why did it matter to him that St George hadn't even kissed her goodbye as they'd left that morning? Why had he even noticed? It hadn't bothered him before on the jet, but it was bothering him now, and he couldn't work out what his problem was.

Surely it should be irrelevant to him where she stayed? As long as her absence didn't affect Simon, it shouldn't affect him.

But that anger wouldn't leave him alone. And the way she was standing there staring at him, so coolly self-possessed, made him want to go over there and do…something. Turn those grey eyes of hers hot. Make her pale, creamy skin go pink. Affect her the way she was affecting him.

Jealous. You're jealous.

His muscles felt tight, his jaw ached. His hands curled into fists under his arms.

Impossible. He wasn't jealous. He had nothing to be jealous about. She was right. Four years had passed since she'd left him on the island so, why any of this should still matter to him, he had no idea.

'I'm not jealous,' he said coldly, ignoring the way the lie sat on his tongue. 'I couldn't care less about what you do with your husband. My only concern is Simon.'

'As if that's not what I think about all the time.' The words echoed sharply between them, a slight wash of pink staining her cheeks.

So. Was he getting to her after all?

'Except when it came to telling your son about his father,' he said, twisting the knife a little further, because he could. Because he wanted her to suffer. To hurt the way he'd been hurt.

'No,' she said steadily, her head held high. 'I was thinking of him then too.'

'Lies. You were thinking of yourself.'

The pink in her cheeks deepened into red, but she didn't flinch. 'Maybe you're right. Maybe I was. But everything I did, I did for him.' There was a quiet strength to the words, a glimpse of steel in her grey eyes.

Whether it was actually true or not, she believed it. The respect he'd felt for her back in England returned, bringing along with it a sense of unease.

Haven't you learned anything? Only a petty man takes his anger out on a woman.

A petty man like his father, for example? Yes, well, the problem with his father was that he had no control over his emotions. He let them rule him.

Enzo did not. He was aware of the danger of turning into Luca Cardinali. So he'd taken those same emotions and, unlike his father, he'd honed them. Turned them into a single-minded determination *not* to be like him.

He'd channelled his own anger, selfishness and greed, and all the other things his mother had accused him of, into building his empire. And he'd done it. Now he was channelling them into making a home for himself and his son.

He had no need to take them out on Matilda.

Which meant he couldn't let her get to him. Couldn't let himself give in to the rage he felt about those lost years without his son. Or the anger at how she'd left him, even though that shouldn't have any power over him.

He had to be cold and hard. Distant. He had to be controlled.

'And so you should,' he said, keeping his voice icy. 'You are quite welcome to stay here in the villa for as long as you want. I'm happy to provide anything you might need.'

Her eyelashes fluttered, clearly caught off-guard by the change in subject and the formality with which he'd said it. 'Thank you.' Her tone was just as formal and distant as his. 'I would prefer to stay here with Simon, if that's okay with you.'

'Certainly.' Enzo pushed himself away from the doorframe. 'Though I would prefer not to host your husband if he comes to visit.'

She blinked again, as if the thought had never occurred to her, which was interesting. Didn't she want to be with him? Sleep with him? Strange, when he knew what a passionate woman she was.

'No,' she said, her voice gone a little husky. 'Of course not. And I expect the same of you. Any... girlfriends of yours need to be kept away from our son.'

Our son. *Our* son.

The words were a hot jolt of electricity.

He gritted his teeth, shoving away the sensation and concentrating instead on the other word. Girlfriends.

Because of course he would have girlfriends. Just because he was a father, didn't mean he was going to be celibate. And, anyway, he'd always wanted a wife at some point, the start of his own family that would be part of the home he wanted to build for himself.

He'd just keep any likely wife candidates away

from Simon until he'd settled on the right one. Which wouldn't be for a while, as he wanted to get to know his son before he made any other plans.

'Naturally,' he said stiffly. 'Though I will be marrying at some point and my future wife will of course meet Simon and be expected to treat him as one of her own.'

Matilda's eyes widened. 'Your future wife?'

'You look surprised. Surely you remember what I told you that night by the fire on the beach?' He shouldn't bring it up. Shouldn't mention that night and what they'd shared. Not when he'd already mentioned it once on the trip to Milan.

Abruptly, she looked away, the deep pink in her cheeks fading, leaving her skin pale, the scattering of freckles stark. 'Yes. I remember.'

Yes, and he'd been very clear about what he wanted in a partner. Too clear. Giving her a list of the qualities that he was sure she couldn't mistake: all qualities he'd seen in her.

And yet the next day she'd disappeared.

'You're just like your father. You're greedy, Enzo.'

That was what his mother had told him in those dark months after they'd been exiled. He'd seen how unhappy she was and had tried to make things better for her, even though he hadn't really known how. He'd helped her clean the tiny apartment, had brought her flowers, had looked after Dante when she'd needed space. But nothing had worked. She'd simply pulled away from him even further.

'I don't know what you want from me,' she'd

*snapped, irritated by his clumsy attempts to make
her smile. 'Whatever it is, I haven't got it.'*

'I want you to be happy,' he'd told her. 'That's all.'

*She'd just looked at him. 'You want too much.
You always have.'*

And, on that island once again, he'd wanted too
much. Demanded more. And she hadn't been able
to handle it. He should never have said anything.

A curious silence fell between them, weighted
and heavy with the past.

He wanted to leave, and yet he couldn't, unable
to look away from her. She was different now from
what she'd been on the island, quieter and far more
contained. Except, when she'd fought him back in
England, there he'd seen that strength blaze, catching fire from the passion he knew lurked inside her.
It was there still, he could sense it. But now it burned
behind a glass wall, the flames bright but without
heat.

He didn't like that. Not one bit.

You want that fire. You want it to burn you again.

He shouldn't. He really shouldn't.

'I thought one day it might be you,' he said before
he could stop himself.

'Who might be me?'

'My future wife.'

She'd gone statue-still, her expression a mask,
half-turned away from him. Her whole posture was
stiff with tension and he had the sense that he'd hurt
her somehow, though why that would be he had no
idea. If she'd truly wanted to be his wife, or even

thought that there might be more for them than a couple of days, she would have stayed. But she hadn't. She'd left. And that had been her decision, not his. If she was hurt then that was her own fault.

Except the thought sounded wrong inside his head, like a justification, and he didn't like that either.

Control, remember? You're not supposed to be petty.

He'd taken a couple of steps towards her before he'd even thought about it, driven by something he didn't understand.

She didn't move. The sun was collecting in her hair, turning it into fire, and he suddenly wanted to touch it, wind that softness around his fingers, have her turn to him, smiling, the way she'd done down on the sand in the darkness, her eyes full of starlight.

Except he couldn't touch her. He couldn't touch her hair or put his hands on her shoulders to soothe her. He couldn't do anything but use words to exorcise his anger and cut her to shreds.

Petty, petty man.

'But you were gone,' he said hoarsely, not really sure why he was continuing with this nonsense. 'You left before we could find out.'

Matilda slowly turned to face him, her eyes gone a dark, steely grey, her hair a blazing coronet in the sun. Her mouth was a hard line and he wanted to take her determined chin and tip her head back, cover that mouth, make it go soft and yielding under his. Taste the fire inside her.

But of course he couldn't, even if he hadn't been controlling himself. That fire wasn't his to taste. She was another's.

'Good thing I did leave.' Her voice was very calm, very steady. 'Because I didn't want to be your wife. In fact, that was the very last thing on earth I wanted.'

He might have believed her if he hadn't seen the glitter in her eyes or the stiff way she was holding herself, the tight angle of her jaw and the slant of her chin.

She was lying. And in leaving she'd denied both of them what they could have had.

Just like she'd denied him his son.

It wasn't supposed to matter. *She* wasn't supposed to matter. And yet the need to do something, anything, became almost overwhelming, and he'd reached out and taken her chin in his hand before he was even aware he'd done it.

She went still, her eyes widening, and all he could think about was how soft her skin felt. How silky and warm. How delectable her mouth was and how badly he wanted to kiss it. Taste it.

How much he wanted to punish her for leaving him, for taking his son and hiding him away. Punish her in a way that would both satisfy her and wreck her, devastate her with pleasure so that she knew exactly what she'd thrown away.

A moment passed, the air shivering around them electric with tension.

He could hear her breathing, fast and erratic, as

she stared at him, her pupils dilating, the grey of her eyes growing darker.

But there was a fire deep in them and it was blazing hot.

He should let her go. He should. She wasn't his to touch, not like this.

Except her skin was so warm and felt like satin and he couldn't stop his thumb from stroking across it. Desire gathered inside him, getting hotter, reflecting the same heat he saw in her eyes.

'You shouldn't tell lies, *cara*.' His voice was roughened and dark. 'Not when I know how to make you tell the truth.'

She didn't pull away, only met him stare for stare. 'And how exactly would you do that?'

It was a challenge and every part of him wanted to take it.

He was hard and ready, and the bed was right there. She wouldn't protest. She'd take him the way she'd taken him back on the island, with fire and passion, as fierce for him as he'd been for her.

But he couldn't. She was another man's wife and that was a line he would not cross.

'I wish I could show you. But I can't.' He had to make himself release her and step away, struggling to ignore the sweet heat of her body and the scent of jasmine that wound around him. 'You're already married. In case you'd forgotten.'

Colour ebbed and flowed in her cheeks, making her eyes glow even brighter. She made no move towards him, but her quickened breathing told him everything he needed to know.

No matter what she said about her husband, she still wanted him.

'I haven't forgotten.' Her voice was husky and her gaze kept dipping to his mouth, as if she couldn't help herself. 'Perhaps I only wanted to see if you had.'

So was that what this was? A test? And, if so, of what?

His groin ached and the need inside him showed no signs of abating. And the way she kept pushing him was only going to end up with one result if he stayed in this room any longer.

So he said nothing, merely turned and left her standing there before he forgot himself and did something he'd regret.

The next few days passed with agonising slowness for Matilda.

Enzo absented himself from the villa, leaving early every morning for Milan, not coming home till late every night presumably to manage his billion-dollar property company.

She would have thought he'd forgotten about Simon if she hadn't stumbled out of bed early the first morning, intending to see how her son was, only to find him sitting with Enzo in the kitchen.

Enzo was dressed in dark suit trousers and a white shirt, and was sitting next to Simon at the scrubbed wooden kitchen table, eating eggs and toast that clearly he'd made, and chatting to his son as if he'd been doing it all his life.

It had made something in Matilda's chest ache seeing them like that, Enzo's focus entirely on Simon as the boy chattered away about racing cars, horses and pools.

She didn't want to interrupt them, so she crept back to bed, thinking she'd go back to sleep. Except she didn't go back to sleep. She lay there in her curtained bed and stared at the canopy above her, replaying the sound of Enzo's voice in her head, full of warmth as he'd talked to their child. A warmth she remembered.

There was no doubt that Enzo wanted him, and not just because he was his, but because he wanted to get to know the boy. It should have made her feel good, but it didn't. All she felt was guilty.

Over the course of the next few days Enzo had breakfast with his son every morning, leaving Matilda to have a few precious hours to herself. She thought she'd enjoy it, but she didn't.

Not when there was nothing to do but think.

She tried to distract herself by exploring the villa, poking around in the old library and the bookshelves full of interesting books, or staring at the paintings on the walls of the dining room. She wondered if they were of Enzo's family—he hadn't told her much about them on the island, only that he had a brother—but she couldn't see any resemblance in the pictures.

Of course, what she should have been doing was picking up the phone and calling Henry, telling him what was happening with Simon, but she hadn't been able to bring herself to do it, mainly because she didn't know what to say.

That she was staying in Italy to be with her son was certain. But how that would affect her marriage to Henry, she had no idea.

She was afraid; she had to admit that to herself. Afraid that he'd be angry with her for going back on her word to be his companion. Afraid that he'd insist that she stay in England. But the thing she was more afraid of was that he'd simply shrug his shoulders and tell her to do whatever she thought best. As if she didn't matter to him any more.

As if he didn't want her.

He might not. But Enzo does.

That thought stayed with her, plagued her for days. That moment in her bedroom when he'd touched her for the first time in four years.

She'd been an idiot to push him, to goad him the way she had, but she hadn't been able to help it. He'd told her that he wanted to marry and that, once, he'd wanted to marry her. And that had hurt. It had *hurt*. As he must have known it would.

Because she hadn't realised, when he'd said all those things about the qualities he'd wanted in a wife, that he'd been talking about her. And why would she? No one else had ever thought those things about her so what had made him different?

So she'd told him that she'd never wanted to

be his wife anyway, because she'd been made of nothing but hurt, and then he'd reached out and taken her chin in his hand. And, the moment his fingers had touched her skin, she hadn't been able to breathe.

His golden eyes had blazed and she'd felt herself catch fire, every inch of her coming alive in a way she hadn't for far too long. Making her aware of how lonely she'd been, and how cold. How badly she'd been starved for touch, because no one touched her these days. No one but her son.

You don't want just anyone to touch you. You want him.

Matilda tried not to think about that as she busied herself during the day with Simon. She took him for walks in the woods and swims in the long, beautifully tiled swimming pool. She thought Henry might try to contact her, but he didn't, leaving her with only a deafening silence.

It made her feel isolated and very, very alone.

But she couldn't let it go on. She'd learned her lesson with Enzo; she couldn't let her fear get in the way of doing what was right.

So, five days after arriving at Enzo's villa, she finally gathered her courage to call Henry. She left it until the evening, after she'd put Simon to bed, and then went and sat on the butter-soft leather sofa in the old library, her phone in one shaking hand as she pressed the call button.

Henry answered after a couple of rings. 'Matilda?' He sounded pleased, with music and people talking loud in the background. 'I've been wondering what was happening. How's Simon?'

'He's good.'

'And you? When can I expect you home?'

She swallowed. 'Well, that's the thing. Enzo wants to keep Simon with him in Italy for a while.'

There was a pause down the other end of the phone, the music and laughter continuing.

'I see,' Henry said after a moment. His voice betrayed nothing. 'I wondered if something like that would happen. Cardinali isn't a man who gives up easily.'

'No,' she agreed. 'He doesn't.'

'So what does that mean for you? Are you going to stay in Italy, then?'

The question sounded casual, as if it didn't matter to him either way.

'I don't have much of a choice.' She tried not to let the hurt show in her voice. 'I could fight him for custody, but...'

'But you're not going to do that.' Henry was firm. 'We don't need that and neither does Simon. Is he happy?'

'Yes,' Matilda said, because she couldn't lie about that, not to Henry. 'He is.'

'Then he's where he belongs.'

She gripped the phone tighter. 'So...what about us?'

'Us?' For a second there was only puzzlement in his voice. 'Oh, right. Well, what do you want to do?'

The question made her chest feel tight. Was he really going to make her choose? Did he not even care enough to state a preference?

He never married you for love, idiot. What do you want from him?

She wanted him to be sorry that she was going to stay in Italy. She wanted him to tell her to come home, even though she wouldn't.

She wanted to know that the four years she'd spent with him had meant something, even if it was just friendship.

'I don't know, Henry,' she said thickly. 'We're supposed to be married. I mean, that's what you wanted, wasn't it?'

There was another silence.

'Yes,' he said at last. 'I did. But it's a little difficult to be married when you're going to be in Italy.' Another pause. 'Not that we had a real marriage anyway.'

'What are you saying?'

Henry sighed. 'Look, you never wanted to marry me in the first place, and I know that. You did it for your aunt and uncle, and I appreciate that. But… maybe it's time you found someone else your own age.'

The words sent a strange shock through her. 'So, you don't want me after all?'

'Mattie.' Henry's voice was kind. 'That's not what our marriage was about. Friendship, remember? And that's what I got. But, I have to admit, maybe I want to move on myself now.'

She didn't know why that hurt her. She didn't love him. What did she care? 'You do?'

'I've…met someone,' he said hesitantly. 'Someone my own age. We get on well and I like her very much.'

'Oh.' She couldn't think of what else to say.

'So perhaps it's time to end our little arrangement,' he went on, with more enthusiasm now, not seeming to notice her shock. 'It was good for the both of us four years ago, but I don't think we need it any more. You want to move on with your life and I want to move on with mine.'

'I…'

'Leave all the details to me.' He didn't wait for her to finish. 'I'll get it all sorted out. I can pull a few strings to make things move a little quicker, get the PR people onto it to make sure there's no press backlash, that kind of thing.'

He said it so quickly it was almost as if he'd been preparing for this moment for quite some time. And maybe he had. Maybe he'd just been waiting for the right time to get rid of her. As her aunt and uncle had got rid of her.

Her throat closed, pain a tight ball in her chest, but she didn't let herself give into it. That wouldn't help anyone, and perhaps this was for the best after all. She could concentrate on being here for Simon and not have to worry about Henry.

'Okay.' She was pleased she sounded so calm and accepting. 'If that's what you want.'

'It is. And what you want also, I assume.' It wasn't a question.

'Of course.' She gritted her teeth. 'Thank you, Henry.'

'No problem.' There was a burst of noise down the other end of the phone. 'Righto, better go. I'll be in touch.'

Silence fell as he hit the disconnect button.

Matilda stared at the screen. So that was that. After four years. He'd met someone else and now he was letting her go.

So many people let you go.

Henry. Her aunt and uncle. Enzo...

And, as if the thought of him had summoned him up like the bloody devil, the library door opened and Enzo strode in.

The sheer impact of his presence, after days without having caught more than a glimpse of him, was like an electric shock delivered straight to her heart.

He was in a dark charcoal suit with a plain white shirt and a silk tie that echoed the gold of his eyes, the sharp, ferocious energy he brought with him everywhere he went flooding the room like static from a thunderstorm.

It made her jerk up in her seat, her breath catching as he shut the door behind him, casually flicking open his suit jacket and shrugging out of it before throwing it over the back of a nearby armchair as he went over to the empty fireplace and stood in front of it.

Matilda put her phone down and tried to calm her

suddenly racing heartbeat. 'You look like you have something to say.'

'You need to prepare Simon for another trip,' Enzo said. 'We'll be leaving next week.'

Yet another shock.

She blinked. 'What? What do you mean, another trip?'

Enzo undid his cufflinks and put them on the mantel above the fireplace then began to fold back one of the sleeves of his shirt, exposing the strong bones of his wrist and the bronze skin of his muscled forearms.

She found herself staring at the movement of his hands, a sudden, intense physical hunger gripping her.

You can touch him now. You're free.

'The island I bought from your husband,' Enzo said, as if he hadn't noticed her staring. 'Isola Sacra. There's an estate on it that I've been in the process of preparing for our eventual arrival. Luckily it didn't need much in the way of work.'

Oh, God, the island. He'd mentioned he'd bought it the day they'd flown to Milan, but she'd forgotten about it.

'Oh,' she said, forcing her gaze from his hands. 'I see.'

'Yes, I'm sure you do. Will you be joining us there? You're most welcome to, though you might prefer to stay on the mainland.' He paused, his eyes glinting. 'Or even go back to England. I'm sure your husband must be missing you.'

The comment slid under her skin like a piece of glass, sharp and painful. As she was sure he'd meant it to. Though, of course, he didn't know that Henry hadn't missed her. Not when he'd had someone else.

'Yes, he is,' she said, goaded. 'He wants me home.'

The glint in Enzo's eyes became a glitter, making her breath catch. He began to roll up his other sleeve, his movements slow; clearly he'd noticed her staring after all. 'And what have you told him so far? Does he know that you're going to stay here with Simon? With me?'

There was no mistaking the emphasis on those last two words, Enzo's gaze making her feel hot and restless, making the hunger inside her deepen.

Yes, he wants you. Unlike Henry.

She met his hungry stare, felt the hot scorch of it over her skin. 'Yes.' Her voice sounded husky. 'He does.'

Enzo stopped rolling up the sleeve of his shirt for a moment, going still, his focus on her narrowing even further.

Tension crackled between them, making her breath catch.

'And he was okay with that?' There was an edge to the words, making them sound like a demand. 'I thought you said he was missing you.'

'He is missing me. But he doesn't tell me what to do. I can make my own decisions.'

Enzo's gaze roved over her as if she was a work of art he'd just bought and he was examining his purchase. 'If you were mine, I'd definitely have something to say about you going and living in another country for four years. With another man.'

If you were mine...

Something trembled inside her. She...could be his. If she divorced Henry, there would be nothing to stop her. And why not? What was there in England for her, when she had to stay in Italy for her son?

And wouldn't it be better that she, rather than some other woman, belonged to Enzo? A woman who would then live with Enzo and Simon, leaving her to be nothing more than a glorified nanny while they became one, big happy family...

No.

The denial rang inside her like a bell. That would happen over her dead body. She wouldn't let another woman be any kind of mother to her child, not while she was alive.

If Enzo wanted a wife then maybe it was time she claimed the position for herself.

CHAPTER SIX

ENZO COULDN'T STOP staring at her. She was sitting on the couch in a soft, floaty dove-grey dress—one of the dresses he'd bought for her—and it matched her eyes, as he'd known it would, making the curls trailing loose over her shoulders gleam like flames. There were little buttons at the neckline and some were open, revealing her pale, creamy skin and the freckles that dusted it. If he flicked a couple more open, he'd expose the tops of her soft, round breasts...

Dio, he shouldn't have come to see her. He should have called her from the office, or sent her a text, or basically anything that involved keeping his distance from her, which was what he'd been trying to do for the past few days.

But, no, he'd assumed that he'd be able to handle it, that his control could withstand her.

Apparently though, all it took was the bright flare of heat in her eyes and that control was shredded all the way through.

Because that was the way she was looking at him right now. With heat, with hunger and not an ounce of fear. The same way she'd looked at him all those years ago.

She'd made a decision about something, clearly. What was it?

'I could be yours.' Her voice was very steady, her gaze level. 'Didn't you say you wanted me to be your wife?'

Of all the things she could have said, *that* was the one thing he hadn't expected, and it took him a moment to process it. 'What do you mean? You're already married.'

'I asked Henry for a divorce.'

Everything stopped.

'A divorce?' His heart was beating hard inside his chest, adrenaline coursing through his body. Because the hunter in him knew what that meant. 'I thought you were in love with him.'

'Perhaps I wasn't…being entirely truthful about that.' Her gaze didn't flicker. 'Perhaps I was only trying to—'

'Make me jealous?' He found he'd taken a step towards her. 'Push me?'

Her chin came up. 'Maybe. The truth is that, for various reasons, Henry and I had a marriage in name only.'

The deep possessiveness that he'd been struggling to keep leashed pulled hard inside him, along with an anger he didn't understand. She'd lied to him about her marriage and why that should matter to him, why he should be angry about it, he had no idea. Because he didn't care. Did he?

'Explain,' he demanded, not bothering to moderate his tone. All his muscles had gone tight, the ever-present need to reach out and grab her almost choking him.

She got up from the sofa, the dress falling around her hips and thighs in a swirl of soft fabric. He wanted to rip it from her body, tear it to shreds and leave it on the floor along with the remains of his control.

But he didn't move. She might have asked for a divorce but that hadn't been granted yet. As far as he was concerned, she was still married. And, aside from anything else, he wasn't going to let that desire inside him free. Not with her. Not again.

'Henry wanted a companion, but he didn't want gossip or scandal about the reasons a young woman would be living with him. So he decided marriage would be a good option.'

'And you agreed? Just like that?'

She lifted one shoulder. 'Why not? He told me he wouldn't touch me and he didn't. I got to live in his house and, when Simon came along, he supported me. But we didn't love each other. We were just friends.'

He studied her face, trying to see if she was spinning more lies. But this sounded like the truth. And it would certainly explain the strange distance he'd observed between her and St George. Not to mention the fact that he hadn't protested when Enzo had dragged her to Italy.

Except…something else was going on here. He could sense it.

'Why are you telling me this?' Enzo took another step towards her even though he hadn't meant to. 'You want something, don't you?'

She held her ground, her chin getting that familiar determined slant. 'I don't want to be here as Simon's glorified nanny. I don't want to stand on the side lines, watching him with a new stepmother, no matter how nice she might be. And I don't want him to be part of anyone's family but mine.' And this time it was she who took a step towards him, that pretty grey dress floating around her, turning her eyes pure silver. 'I'm his mother. Which means, if you want a wife to complete your little family, you need to choose me.'

He wanted to laugh. Who on earth did she think she was to demand such a thing, after what she'd done? Did she really imagine that he'd simply say yes and marry her without any protest whatsoever?

Dio, the audacity of her.

'And what the hell makes you think I'll do anything of the sort?' He smiled at her, hungry and sharp. 'You're the one who left me, *cara*. Do you seriously imagine that I would now come running simply because you asked?'

She took another step, getting right into his space, the soft heat of her body and the sweet scent of jasmine clouding his senses. He was getting hard, his pulse accelerating. He hadn't had a woman since he'd first seen her in England, and not for weeks before then either, and now he felt every single second of that time weighing down on him.

He should have indulged himself while he'd been going to the office every day—he had a few names he could have called, women who'd be happy to see him—but it had felt wrong to do so when Simon was only newly with him.

A stupid decision.

If he'd taken one of those women to bed, maybe he wouldn't be feeling so desperate now.

Liar. It's her. It's always *been her.*

Matilda raised her hand and rested her fingertips lightly on his chest, and he felt her touch echo through him like a bell being struck. Heat gripped him, a raw desire that had the breath catching in his throat,

'You want me, Enzo,' she said quietly. 'And I want you.' Hunger glittered in her eyes, the same that probably blazed in his. 'So why not?'

Yes. Why not?

There were reasons. Such as the fact that he didn't like being told what to do by anyone, let alone a woman who'd first run from him and then hadn't told him that he'd had a son. Who'd lied to him about the state of her marriage, making him feel things he hadn't felt before…things such as jealousy…

Then again, he did want a wife eventually, and it made sense for him to marry her, as Simon already knew and loved her. And Enzo wouldn't have to put him through meeting various women, which would be stressful for all concerned.

And of course the sex with Matilda would be incredible. He would insist on that. There would be no 'marriage in name only' nonsense for him.

But look what happened to your parents' marriage. To your mother. And you're so like your father...

A cold sensation he didn't want to feel twisted in his gut. But he shoved it away.

It didn't matter. He wasn't the same as Luca and neither was Matilda like his mother. And this marriage wouldn't be quite the same. She was free to live her own life; he wouldn't stop her. He wouldn't suck the life out of her like his father had his mother. His feelings were on total lockdown. Desire was all he felt, good, old-fashioned lust, and he could handle that no problem.

So, yes. Why not? Though, there was one thing she'd need to be aware of: this wouldn't be a marriage of a few years. This would be for ever.

He'd lost everything once and, yes, he'd played a part in that. But he would not lose it again.

But it wouldn't do to look too eager. He would make her wait, punish her a little first.

He didn't move, trying not to concentrate on the slight pressure of her fingers on his chest or the fire inside him that she'd ignited. 'What brought this on?'

Her fingers trailed down the cotton of his shirt in a gentle stroke. 'I just don't want to subject my son to an endless parade of women.'

'And I told you already that I would never do that to him.'

'You don't need to do that to him at all.' She lifted

her hand again to the top few buttons of his shirt and flicked them open. 'Not if the endless parade of women consists entirely of me.'

He allowed himself a smile, hungry and white as the material parted and she touched one finger to the bare skin of his throat. Her touch burned like a flame. 'If you're thinking I'm going to be happy with the kind of marriage you had with your Henry, you can think again.' His voice had become rougher, deeper. 'You will sleep in my bed beside me every night. And when I say sleep, I mean that you will be naked and I will be inside you.'

A flush stained her lovely skin, her gaze on her finger where it rested against his throat. 'I know. I want that too.'

'You will not take lovers, *cara*. It will be me and only me, which means this is for ever, Matilda. Are you sure you're ready for that?'

Enzo's smooth, bronze skin was a hot coal beneath her fingertip and she could feel the beat of his pulse, strong, sure and steady.

He was so close, his body radiating heat like a fire, the hard muscles of his chest visible between the parted fabric of his shirt.

If she moved just a bit closer, the tips of her breasts would be brushing against him.

The thought made her shudder, her nipples suddenly hard and aching.

The delicious spice of his aftershave was making it difficult to think about much of anything but the hunger that seemed to pulse in time with his heartbeat.

To be his wife. To be his for ever.

It wasn't a surprise that he'd said that, and she had to be honest with herself: part of her had known that was what he'd wanted back there on the island and, deep down, she knew that was why she'd run from him. Because she hadn't been ready for a man like him, not then.

She didn't know whether she was ready for a man like him now.

He'd been so demanding back then, drawing from her all the heat and passion she had to give, and then some. But even that hadn't been enough for him. It had felt like he'd wanted her soul as well, but she hadn't been ready to give it. She'd been too afraid of his intensity. Too afraid of the intensity of her own feelings too, especially after the emotional desert in which she'd grown up with her aunt and uncle. They'd always been emotionally reserved and after her parents' deaths they'd only become more so.

No one had talked to her about feelings or how to manage them.

No one had talked to her at all.

Being with Enzo, with all his ferocity, had been scary and she'd had no one to talk to about it. She'd never missed her mother more.

Matilda could feel the pressure of his gaze on her like a breath of flame. Looking into it would probably burn her alive so she kept her attention on the white cotton of his business shirt instead.

He was fierce now, but she knew it wasn't like it had been four years ago. His intensity was purely to do with their sexual chemistry. And, when he'd said it would be for ever, it wasn't because he loved her.

A small part of her shivered at that thought, but she ignored it.

She'd done without love for most of her adult life and she could survive the lack. And there would be consolations, after all.

'Well?' His rich, dark voice rolled over her like black velvet. 'What's it to be?'

Consolations such as his hot, smooth skin beneath her finger. She couldn't stop herself from running the tip of it down from the hollow of his throat to the hard muscle of his chest.

No, for ever wouldn't be so bad. Not if she could have this.

You couldn't handle him then. What makes you think you can handle him now?

Easy. If there was no emotion involved then she'd do just fine.

And, anyway, this wasn't about her and her fears. Simon needed her. He needed a father. He needed a family. And she couldn't deny him the chance of one.

'For ever is a long time.' She couldn't stop staring at the contrast of the pale skin of her finger against the bronzed muscle of his chest. 'Are you sure that's what you want?'

'If you're in my bed, what more could I possibly need?' The rough sound in his voice made her go hot all over. 'I have lost too many things, *cara*. I will not lose anything more.'

She swallowed and forced herself to look at him, forced herself not to be such a coward. And she had to catch her breath as the brilliant amber of his gaze hit her, surrounding her.

There was no mercy in that look, just as she'd suspected there wouldn't be. No softness. Only fire. Only hunger. He wasn't going to give a single inch of ground. It was all or nothing with Enzo and it always had been.

A small flame of anger burst to life inside her at him and how he'd somehow taken control of the situation. And at herself for the way she let him do it.

'So I'm just a thing to you?' She didn't bother keeping the sharpness from her voice. 'No one wants to be just a thing, Enzo.' Certainly she didn't. That was all she'd been to her aunt and uncle, a thing that they'd inherited, that they hadn't wanted. And it was all she'd been to Henry too because, for all his assertions about wanting a companion, he'd still bought her.

'And what more do you want?' The ferocity in his expression just about ate her alive. 'I was prepared to give you everything four years ago, but you left. You had your chance, Summer. That deal is now no longer on the table.'

A whiplash of pain curled down her spine. Damn him for using that name against her. Damn him for even bringing up their affair in the first place.

But she'd told herself in England that she needed

to armour herself against him so she didn't let the hurt show, allowing the flame of her anger to grow higher, hotter, instead.

She wasn't going to let him have control of the situation. Not here. Not now.

Holding the scorching heat of his gaze, Matilda slowly pressed her palm down on his bare chest between the two halves of his shirt and spread all five fingers out on his bare skin. 'Good,' she said clearly, letting him see the challenge in her eyes. 'Because I didn't want that deal anyway. All I want from you is this.' And she stroked him with her thumb, a long, slow caress.

He didn't move, but his muscles went tight and hard beneath her palm.

He smiled his tiger's smile and her heart fluttered in her chest, a strange combination of fear and excitement tangling inside her.

Meet him on his own ground? You might as well try to rope a hurricane...

The doubt pricked at her, but she shoved it away before it could settle.

He wanted her, of that there was no question. Time to use that power to her own advantage.

'Then we're agreed.' A thread of dark sensuality ran through his voice, raising goose bumps all over her skin. 'But if you're expecting *this* right now you're going to be disappointed. You're still another man's wife, in case you've forgotten.' He lifted a hand, his fingers circling her wrist, pressing lightly against the sensitive skin on the underside of it, resting on her pulse. The scorching heat of his touch nearly made her gasp. 'And you know what that means, don't you? It means I won't touch you until your divorce comes through.' But he didn't release her. His fingers tightened fractionally instead, the heat in his eyes becoming a blaze. 'But maybe you need a reminder of exactly who you're dealing with when it comes to making bargains with me.'

She didn't understand what he was talking about until he guided her own hand to her throat, letting her fingertips settle on the skin above the neckline of her dress. 'This is where I will touch you, Matilda.'

A shiver went through her, the sound of her pulse loud in her ears.

She should pull her hand away, not let him tease her like this, because she knew what this was: he was taking control again. But…she couldn't seem to make herself move. Every inch of her skin felt alive and acutely sensitive, and she wanted more.

So she went still as he eased her hand down, trailing her fingers over the fabric, following the swell of her breast, watching her with that intense, sharp focus. 'Then maybe here.'

Her mouth went dry.

He shifted her hand again, her fingertips brushing lightly over one tight, hard nipple, making pleasure arc through her, sweet and sharp, tearing a gasp from her throat.

His eyes were molten as he shifted her hand once more to her other breast, letting her fingers brush her nipple again. 'Next time, though, it'll be my hand.'

The rough, sensual promise in the words was like a caress in itself. 'My fingers touching you.'

She shuddered as another intense jolt of pleasure washed through her, knowing that all she had to do to stop him from stealing her power was to pull away.

Except…she didn't want to. And that was the pleasure and the agony of it. There was something inside her, hungry, greedy and demanding. The part of her that he'd woken all those years ago, the part she'd put on ice when she came back to England.

And now it was awake again. Now it was aware of everything it had been missing and now it *wanted*…

Enzo stepped closer, the heat of his body surrounding her, the sharp, musky scent of male arousal threaded through with her own making her dizzy. And he moved her hand from her breast, easing it down over her stomach, down further, guiding it between her legs to where the pulse of her desire beat so strong and hard.

A low moan escaped her as her own fingers brushed the sensitive place hidden beneath the cotton of her dress and her underwear. Just lightly. A tease.

'And I will touch you here too,' he went on in that dark, soft voice. 'Make you even wetter for me than you are already, hmm?'

'Enzo…' His name breathed out of her on a sigh.

'Yes, *cara*. You will say my name just like that.' He covered her hand with his, holding her fingers down, his strength irresistible. 'Again. Say it again. *Now*.' And he adjusted the pressure so that the tip of her finger pressed against that sensitive place between her thighs, making pleasure flare along every nerve ending she had.

'*Enzo...*' she gasped, helplessly obeying as the intensity of the sensation shivered through her.

A very male kind of satisfaction glittered in his eyes. 'Yes, that's good.' He kept the slight pressure on her finger right where it was. 'But I won't give you everything you want right when you want it. Because, remember, not only did you lie to me about Simon but you lied to me about your marriage. You made me believe it was something it wasn't and I can't allow that.' He shifted his hand slightly, yet another blade of pleasure piercing her. 'So I have an extra term for our deal. If you want me to make you come, *cara mia*, you will have to beg me for it.'

Shudders racked her, but she forced them back, trying to concentrate on what he was saying. 'So this is a punishment? That's what you're saying, isn't it? I wouldn't have thought you'd care.'

'I didn't think I would either.' He pressed a little harder, making her groan. 'Turns out I do. But don't worry. I think you'll enjoy the kind of punishments I give out. In fact, I guarantee it.'

The sound of her accelerated breathing was loud in the silence of the room, along with the echo of her pulse thundering in her head. Her skin was burning, the damp heat of her own arousal soaking through her dress against her fingertips.

She should be ashamed at how easily she was letting him manipulate her like this, but all she could think about was how much she wanted him to touch her bare skin, to stroke her and never stop.

'No, there will be no begging,' she forced out through gritted teeth. 'Unless you're the one on your knees.'

He only laughed softly. 'If I'm on my knees, then I know where my mouth will be. And it won't be begging you for anything. It will be occupied with making you scream.'

The fire in her cheeks burned hotter, the throb between her thighs more intense. She wanted to tell him that there would be no screaming either, but her voice wouldn't work.

Then abruptly his hand dropped away and he stepped back.

'Enzo,' she breathed, not able to stop from saying his name.

He only gave her one long, sweeping look as she stood there swaying, barely able to stand upright, her own hand still tucked between her thighs. 'I know, you want it now, don't you? Sadly for both of us, you're still married.' He didn't smile, though there was something dark and possessive in his eyes. 'Let me know when your divorce comes through. We'll continue this discussion then.'

And, before she could say another word, he turned and swept out.

CHAPTER SEVEN

'A SON YOU didn't know about?' Dante's voice was ever so slightly incredulous. 'Surely that's something that would happen to me, not you?'

Enzo kept his attention on the big plate-glass windows in front of him, gazing out over the Milanese skyline.

His Milan office was his favourite, mainly because whenever he looked out of the windows and gazed over the city beneath him it felt as if he was sitting on a throne, the city he'd once struggled to find a place in now at his feet.

It was a very satisfying feeling.

'Yes, well, I'm surprised it hasn't happened to you already,' Enzo said, clasping his hands behind his back. 'Given your apparent inability to spend even one night without a woman in your bed.'

'Is that the subtle note of judgement I hear, brother mine?' Dante asked lazily. 'Or is it hypocrisy instead?'

Enzo allowed himself a smile, the reflection in the glass smiling along with him. His brother took pleasure in baiting him, though Enzo didn't let it bother him, as it was never personal. Dante took pleasure in baiting everyone he met, which sometimes wasn't the most desirable trait when he was supposed to be the friendly face of Cardinal Enterprises.

'Simon is four,' Enzo said, ignoring the dig. 'You'll meet him soon.'

'How exciting.' Dante sounded anything but excited at the prospect. 'And you said you're going to marry the boy's mother? After she ran out on you and then hid your son from you?'

Enzo had told him the story of Simon's arrival in coldly clinical terms, touching lightly on his affair with Matilda but not going into it in any depth. He hadn't wanted to tell Dante any sooner, not until he'd firmed up his plans, but now he had those in place it was time to start making announcements.

First his brother, then the rest of the world.

But not until Matilda's divorce had come through. There would be scandal, obviously, but if he handled it right he could keep it to a minimum.

'Yes.' In the glass, he could see his smile turn sharp, remembering Matilda in the library, hot, panting and completely at his mercy. Intoxicating. 'I am.'

'Interesting. I wouldn't have thought forgiveness would be your strong suit.'

'The marriage is not about forgiveness.' Finally, he turned around to face his brother, who was lounging on a low, black leather sofa like a lion sunning itself on a rock. 'The marriage is about my son. She's his mother, which makes her the best choice of wife.'

Just ignore the fact that you want her for yourself.

He wasn't ignoring that. He *did* want her for himself. But only for his bed, nothing more. And, if the thought of meting out a few sensual punishments on her lovely body got him hard, then what of it?

Dante only rolled his eyes. His younger brother didn't much care about a great many things—or at least he professed not to care. He didn't have the same burning need that Enzo did for a home and a family. In fact, as he'd often said to Enzo, a home and a family sounded like hell on earth to him, and he was glad he wasn't a prince any more. All care, no responsibility, that was Dante. And, given Dante's upbringing after their mother had taken him away, Enzo couldn't say he blamed him.

'Your funeral,' Dante said. 'So I presume you're going to introduce me to this paragon at some point?'

Possessiveness flooded through Enzo and he let it, because why not? Matilda was all his now. Then again, it was ridiculous to feel that way, especially about his brother. Dante might be a notorious man whore, but he would never poach on another man's territory, especially not if that man was Enzo.

Still, the idea made Enzo restless.

He paced over to the desk that stood in front of the windows and neatened the stack of papers sitting on it. 'Of course. But not yet. I can't make it public until her divorce is finalised.'

Dante's black brows rose into his hairline. 'Divorce? You mean she's married?'

Enzo would have found his shock amusing if he hadn't been battling the restlessness that had him pacing from the desk, back to the windows and then back to the desk again. 'Yes,' he snapped. 'She's married. No, I haven't touched her. It's a long story.'

'Sounds like it.' Dante's dark eyes glinted with his usual lazy amusement. 'Anything else you want to tell me?'

'No.' Enzo found himself straightening the papers again and had to force himself to stop. 'Haven't you got something else to do?'

Dante held up a hand. 'Hey, you were the one who called this meeting, not me.'

'And now it's over. I'd appreciate you keeping this to yourself until I give the word.' He glared at his brother. 'I don't want the press getting hold of anything, not yet. For my son's sake.'

For a second the bored expression on Dante's handsome face flickered. 'Don't look at me like that,' he said, a thread of warning in his voice. 'Your secret is safe with me, cross my heart and hope to die.'

Dante wouldn't say anything and Enzo knew that. But the protectiveness that gripped him whenever he thought about his son was something he couldn't stop. Nor did he want to.

'Good,' was all he said. 'I'll let you know when it becomes public.'

The door shut behind his brother and Enzo turned once more to the city outside his window. *Dio*, that time had better be soon.

The renovation of the villa on Isola Sacra was almost complete. Once Matilda's divorce came through, he would marry her and then he would move his family onto the island as he'd always envisaged.

Desire, thick and hot, pulsed through him as he remembered her almost swaying on her feet as he'd guided her own hand between her legs that night in the library.

He'd been able to feel the heat of her even with her palm between his hand and her body, the sweet, musky scent of feminine arousal heavy in the air. She'd shivered so beautifully, said his name so desperately. Her eyes had been dark as thunderstorms and yet lightning had glowed in their depths, a glimpse of the passionate, intense woman he'd discovered four years ago on that island.

Enzo gritted his teeth as his body hardened at the memory.

It had taken everything he had to step away from her in that moment, but he'd done it. Because he'd had a point to prove to himself, if not to her: that he was in charge here and he dictated the situation. And if she wanted to test him then she needed to learn just what kind of opponent she was up against. She could not beat him. He would not let her.

She'd told him that St George apparently had paid a few people to make sure the process of dissolving the marriage went quicker, but it had been several weeks at least, and Enzo found that once again he'd had to absent himself from the villa. He made sure he had breakfast with Simon every morning, because that was important in building his relationship with his son, and sometimes he'd come home earlier at night to spend more time with him.

But the real issue was Matilda.

Vowing not to touch her until her divorce had come through had been a good strategic move, and fine in theory, but he was a little appalled at himself at how difficult in practice it actually was.

The scent of jasmine haunted the hallways of his villa and the sound of her voice echoed through the rooms, soft and husky and sensual. It distracted him, made him even more restless than he was already. Even more hungry.

He'd never had a problem with physical desire before, had always found it easy to control, but not now. Not with her.

He was tired of it.

He couldn't stop watching her whenever they met, his gaze irresistibly drawn. She'd stopped wearing the T-shirts and jeans he'd first seen her in and had adopted those floaty dresses that drew attention to her curves, with buttons at the neckline always half-undone and a swirling skirt around her hips that would sometimes, depending on how she was standing, drape seductively around her thighs.

She'd taken to wearing her hair loose too, the flame-red curls drifting across her shoulders and licking around her pale neck.

It was almost as if she knew how the waiting was driving him mad and was determined to make it worse. He wouldn't put it past her. After all, she'd used his own tactics against him that night in the library.

A hot, raw thrill went through him at the thought.

Well, if she was, good. He liked it when she fought him and he thought she probably liked fighting him too.

It would make her eventual surrender all the sweeter for both of them.

There came a buzz from his desk.

He shook himself from his thoughts and paced over to it, hitting the intercom button with some impatience. 'What is it, Alessia?'

'There's someone here to see you.' His secretary sounded disapproving. 'A woman. She wouldn't give me her name.'

Everything inside Enzo tightened instinctively. He didn't know how he knew, but he did. 'Does she have red hair?'

'Yes, as a matter of fact, she does.'

His pulse accelerated. 'Send her in.'

There could only be one woman with red hair who would come to see him without an appointment, and only one reason she'd come to him in his office.

The door opened and in she came, the skirt of her long, flowing white dress billowing out behind her, her hair loose down her back.

Matilda.

He hadn't been this close to her in days and now here she was, filling his office with her delicious scent and her heat…

His hunger sharpened to a knife edge.

'You'd better be here to tell me you're a free woman,' he said, only just masking the growl in his voice. 'Because I'm getting tired of this little game you're playing with me.'

Matilda clasped her hands in front of her so he wouldn't see them shake, the determination she'd found earlier evaporating under the heat of Enzo's intense, hungry focus.

He was standing behind his desk, tall, dark and powerful. Like the king he'd been born to be. He was in one of his beautifully tailored suits, dark charcoal with a black shirt and a tie of rich red silk, and he wore it like he was wearing robes of state. All he needed was a crown on his head and the look would be complete.

But he didn't need a crown, not when his golden eyes blazed like the sun, pinning her to the spot where she stood.

She took a silent, shaken breath.

The papers had come from the courier that morning and she'd stood there a while, staring at them in her hand, an electric kind of excitement pooling in her gut laced with the undeniable bite of fear.

Excitement because she'd been fighting the pull of her chemistry with Enzo and she didn't need to fight it any more. Fear because the second she took the papers to him he would stop fighting it too. And then everything would change.

But you have a plan.

Yes, she did. She'd decided on it the night in the

library after he'd left. If she was going to handle a man like Enzo Cardinali, she was going to need to have some kind of power over him, and she knew exactly what kind of power that was. The only thing she had: their chemistry.

So for the past couple of weeks she'd been wearing the floaty dresses he'd bought for her, with a little bit of skin on show. Enough to tantalise him, tease him, without giving everything away; to test that much-vaunted control of his, show him that she had a power of her own and she was prepared to use it.

And it had worked. His gaze had followed her wherever she went, the hunger in it evident. And, when he'd started to absent himself from her presence more and more, she knew that it wasn't because he didn't want to see her.

She *was* testing him.

It made her feel that maybe a marriage to him wouldn't crush her completely.

So when those papers had come she'd shoved her doubts away and left Simon with Maria, getting his driver to take her directly from the villa to his office. And, as they'd headed into Milan's heavy traffic, she'd held tight to her determination to prove to him that she would not let him walk all over her, to the certainty that she had some power here.

But now as she stood in his office, with only a desk standing between her and the furious masculine hunger that radiated from him, that certainty wavered just a little.

She didn't let it show.

Steeling her spine, she reached for the papers she had in her handbag. 'I don't know what game you're talking about, but you're right. That's exactly why I'm here.' She pulled out the envelope and held it up. 'One divorce. Signed, sealed…' She slowly walked forward to the desk, placing the envelope down on it. 'And delivered.'

Enzo's gaze dropped to the envelope then lifted back to her face again. He didn't move, but the tension already gathering in the air, dense as an electrical storm, thickened even further, making her breath catch hard.

'Lock the door,' Enzo ordered, his voice full of darkness and heat, raising all the hairs on the back of her neck.

Something needy and demanding inside her leapt and abruptly she was conscious of the sweet ache between her legs, the one that had been there ever since he'd touched her in the library and hadn't gone away.

So, he wasn't going to wait.

Good. She was ready.

She turned and went to the doors of his office, locking them with a hand that only shook a little.

'Come here,' he murmured.

She didn't disobey, turning back to him and moving over to the desk, again slowly, letting her skirts swirl around her. The white dress had been a deliberate choice—it was practically see-through. She had to use any and all weapons she could in this particular fight.

His gaze followed her as she came towards him,

the gold flames in his eyes burning, and she held it as she approached the desk and then moved around it to him.

He took a step back, indicating that she should stand between him and the desk, so she did, her heartbeat thudding harder.

The desk was at her back, the edge pressing against the backs of her thighs while he stood in front her, so close, his body lean and powerful, his shoulders blocking the view of Milan through the windows behind him. The sun caught glints of deep blue in his ink-dark hair, throwing the aristocratic planes and angles of his face into shadow. But his eyes were molten and the expression in them made her tremble the way she'd trembled when he'd first looked at her on that island four years ago.

She wanted him. She *wanted* him so badly.

So why fight him?

But she wasn't fighting him. She was letting him have what they both desperately wanted. She only wanted to show him that he wouldn't get to have things all his own way.

He didn't speak; instead his hands settled on her hips and he lifted her onto his desk as if she weighed nothing at all.

Matilda bit down on her instinctive gasp as the heat of his palms burned through the thin cotton of her dress, in stark contrast to the cool wood of the desktop. She couldn't stop looking at him, even though his gaze was scorching her. He was magnetic north and she was a compass needle, relent-lessly pulled towards him and held there, powerless.

But no, she wasn't powerless, was she? Because she could see her own power in his eyes, in the hunger, and beneath that something else, something she remembered back from those long, heated days on the island. When he'd taken her again and again, demanding and ferocious, as if he'd been starving for something that only she'd been able to feed.

She'd never understood what it was that he was starving for, but she could see that same need burning in his expression right now. A kind of desperation.

It made her heart go tight for some reason and before she could think better of it she reached out to cup his hard jaw with her palm, his skin hot against hers. 'It's all right, Enzo,' she said. 'You can have me. Right now, if you want it.'

Shock flared in his eyes, his head jerking back from her touch almost instantly, as if she was the one who'd burned him and not the other way around.

Then, as if he'd realised what he'd done, his mouth pulled back in a snarl, anger blazing. 'You think I would wait?' His hands slid from her hips down her thighs to her knees, his thumbs sliding between them as he gripped them. 'After four years?' Despite the savagery in his eyes, his hands were gentle as he pulled her thighs wide. 'You've been flaunting yourself at me, teasing me for the past two weeks. And now I'm hungry, *cara*. I'm not going to wait.'

The intimate stretch of her inner thigh muscles made her shiver, the throb in her sex more intense. And maybe his obvious anger should have made her afraid, especially considering what they were about to do.

But for some reason it didn't; she knew he wouldn't hurt her. No, it wasn't fear that she felt. Beneath the pull of her own desire was curiosity. A burning need to know why he'd pulled away so sharply from her touch.

She stared up into his beautiful face, trying to ignore the heat of his hands on her. 'Why are you so angry, Enzo?'

He blinked, the question obviously taking him by surprise, but then the shock in his eyes was quickly masked. 'Why do you think?' He gave her a savage kind of smile as his hands curved to grip her just above each knee, his thumbs stroking back and forth along the sensitive skin on the inside of them. 'Because you've been flitting about the villa in see-through dresses, and don't tell me it's just because it's hot outside.'

But Matilda slowly shook her head. 'That's not why you're angry.'

His jaw hardened. 'Oh, no, *cara*. We're not doing this now.' He stroked her inner thighs with his thumbs, sliding higher and higher, and she could feel her curiosity begin to dissolve like fog on a hot day, burned away by the heat of his touch.

Thinking was difficult. Breathing almost impossible. All there was in the entire world was the intense, blazing gold of his eyes and the demand in them. The heat of his body inches from hers and the hot spice of his scent that wrapped itself around her.

'Tell me, Matilda,' Enzo ordered, the timbre of his voice even rougher, even darker, his accent more pronounced. 'Tell me you want this.'

Again, the hint of that desperation in his voice, the hot glitter of it in his gaze. Almost as if he was… afraid that she might not give it to him.

It was a glimpse of vulnerability, a chink in his icy armour, and it hooked into something deep inside her.

She could use that vulnerability against him, the way he used her vulnerabilities against her. Or… she could do something else. Show him something better.

He was a man who loved a fight; she knew that by now. And he was used to it. He fought his battles in the boardroom every day. But what if he didn't have to fight to have her? What if she simply…gave herself to him? Surrendered completely, the way she had on the island?

Matilda didn't think too hard about it, she simply went with her instinct, putting her hands on the desk behind her and leaning back on them, conscious of how the posture arched her spine and lifted her breasts. 'I want this,' she said huskily, letting her own desire show in her gaze. 'I want *you*.'

The bright gold in his eyes flared, then slowly he leaned forward, placing his hands near hers so his body was looming over her, his gaze mere inches away. 'You know I'll make you beg, don't you? I promised you I would.'

A shiver coursed down her spine. Even fully dressed the heat he put out astonished her, making everything inside her want to burn along with him. The need to touch him, put her hands to his chest and test all the hard muscle beneath his shirt, was almost overwhelming.

But she held back, teasing them both a little. 'I did tell you there would be no begging involved.'

The intensity in his face became as sharp as a sword blade. He leaned in a fraction more until his mouth was almost brushing hers. 'And I told you what would happen if I got down on my knees for you.' His breath was warm and smelled of peppermints and she wanted to kiss him so badly she couldn't think. 'Are you sure you're ready for that?'

She swallowed, the wild thrill of him, of the surrender she was going to give him, making her brave in a way she'd never imagined. 'Of course. Perhaps you should stop talking and start doing.'

For a second he said nothing, merely stared intently at her.

Then he reached down, gripped her thighs and pulled her to the edge of the desk.

Matilda's heartbeat was drumming in her head and she couldn't control her breathing. He was looking at her as if he wanted to eat her alive.

You know that's probably what he's going to do.

Oh, yes, she did. And she couldn't wait.

She trembled as he dropped to his knees in front of the desk and reached to push the fabric of her skirt up and around her waist, baring her but for the small scrap of white lace between her legs.

The aristocratic lines of his face tightened, naked hunger glittering in his eyes as he stared at her for one long second. Then he hooked a finger in the lace of her knickers and pulled them to the side, exposing her completely.

She couldn't stop shaking, little shivers chasing over her skin. She loved the way he looked at her; it made her want to spread her legs wider for him.

'Beautiful,' he murmured, his gaze directly on the small cluster of damp curls. 'Exactly like I remembered. Red as fire and just as hot.' His hands slid up the outside of her thighs then slipped beneath them, drawing her even closer to the edge of the desk, right to where his mouth was.

Her own breathing was becoming frantic. She put her hands out to grip the edge of the desk, holding on tight, because the second he put his mouth to her she was going to go up in flames.

Then Enzo's fingers were tightening on her thighs, his thumbs moving over her slick flesh, spreading her open, his hot breath feathering over her sensitive sex and making her shudder.

Then his mouth covered her, his tongue pushing inside her, and she was lost.

The pleasure was sharp, agonising, and she groaned with sheer relief because at last—*at last*—he was touching her and it had been so long since she'd been touched, so long since she'd felt any kind of physical pleasure that the intensity of the sensation was almost a shock.

She wanted to look down, to see what he was doing, but that would probably push her over the edge and she didn't want this to end, not so soon.

So she closed her eyes and reached for him, threaded her fingers through the black silk of his hair, shifting her hips against his mouth, wanting even more intensity, even more sensation.

But his hands closed hard on her hips, holding her in place so she couldn't move. 'Keep still,' he said roughly. 'Or you won't get what you want.'

She shuddered. 'Enzo, please...'

'Yes, that's a good start.' He leaned in again, breathing over her, making her tremble. 'Beg me in Italian and I'll give you more.'

Her brain wouldn't work. What was 'please' in Italian? She couldn't remember. 'I don't...kn-know.'

'You do, *cara*. I taught you, remember? You used to say it so beautifully.' His thumbs moved, stroking over her flesh, giving her pleasure in short, hard jolts. 'Perhaps you need a reminder?'

But no, she remembered now. She remembered completely. '*Per favore*, Enzo...' she whispered, her fingers tightening further in his hair.

'Good girl,' he murmured. 'Now scream for me.'

And she felt his mouth on her again, his tongue exploring her wet flesh, his fingers stroking her, taking her apart with ecstasy, and then there was no thought at all.

She surrendered completely.

When he pushed his tongue inside her one final time, she did scream.

Just as he wanted her to.

CHAPTER EIGHT

HIS OFFICE ECHOED with the sound of his name as Matilda shuddered and came apart in his hands, the sweet taste of her climax against his tongue. And no doubt his secretary would have heard it too.

Enzo didn't care.

The only thing that mattered was the woman shaking on the desk in front of him, her warm body in his arms, the flavour of her in his mouth.

Dio, finally.

After all the years when she'd haunted his dreams, here she was at last. On his desk, in his arms. His. As she was always meant to be.

He stroked his hands down her bare thighs, caressing her as she trembled. Then he reached for the waistband of her knickers and began to draw them down and off her.

His heart was beating fast and he was so hard he hurt. But he wasn't going to rush this. He wasn't going to let her dictate the way this would go.

He wanted to punish her for what she'd done to him, for every second of the four years since she'd left him, for all the lies she'd told him and for what she continued to do to him with her very existence, driving him to madness.

Yes, he would punish her.

With pleasure.

He got to his feet, tugging her underwear completely free then discarding it on the floor. She didn't move, looking up at him from beneath her lashes, her skin flushed a deep pink, her eyes gone silver and glazed with heat. His very own, sexy, sultry siren.

He slid one hand into her silky red hair and took it in his fist, then he gently eased her head back so those soft, full lips were near his. Then he covered them with his, pushing his tongue into her mouth, exploring the sweet heat of her and letting her taste herself on him.

She shuddered, a soft moan escaping her throat. Her arms lifted and she wound them around his neck, beginning to kiss him back, hesitant at first and then hungrier, more demanding.

Yes, this was the woman he remembered. The one who'd kept nothing back and met him passion for passion. Giving him everything without reservation. Making him want more, so much more…

Careful.

He caught his breath. Yes, he did have to be careful, not let himself get out of hand. He could not let her generous passion get to him the way it had all those years ago.

This time he'd stay in control.

He tightened his grip on her hair and kissed her

harder as he reached into his back pocket for his wallet. Then he nipped at her lower lip, gentle bites that made her tremble, before he released her and stepped back.

Her cheeks were even more flushed, her mouth full and red from his kiss. The air was heavy with the scent of jasmine and the sweet, musky smell of her arousal. It was incredibly erotic. It made him want to spread her out over his desk and taste her again, maybe this time spending a couple of hours making her gasp and cry and scream his name.

But he was so hard and he ached, and his patience was at an end.

He pulled out a condom, then casually discarded his wallet on the desk.

She reached out for it, reminding him of how he'd once shown her how to roll the latex down onto him and how she'd much enjoyed doing it. Not to mention how much he'd enjoyed her cool fingers on him.

But not now. He was in charge of this, not her.

'You want to help, then get me out,' he ordered, unable to keep the rough edge from his voice.

Her gaze met his. 'You don't have to fight me, Enzo,' she said, reaching to undo his belt then flick open the button on his trousers. 'Not now. I'll do whatever you want.'

He stilled. There was a gentleness to her voice that hadn't been there before, a warmth that flowed over him like honey. A gentleness he remembered from the island, that had reached inside his chest and wrapped itself around his heart. He'd never had gentleness. His mother had never been demonstrative even before they'd been exiled, and afterwards nothing he could do was right. He'd never had warmth from her, only rejection. And after she'd gone there had only been the ice of his father's bitterness and indifference.

That was your fault and you know it. If you hadn't been so demanding...

The thought drifted through his head, but he shoved it away. Grabbed for the anger that always came so willingly, so easily.

Except anger was hard to hold onto when her fingers were clutching the zip of his fly and slowly drawing it down, the slight brush of her knuckles against his hard-on nearly undoing him.

You don't want to fight her either.

Another unwelcome thought, though this one he couldn't seem to get rid of. It stayed there as she tried to slip her cool fingers into his boxers, and he found himself letting her, the touch of her hand around his swollen flesh making him groan.

Dio, she was going to undo him completely if he let her keep touching him like this.

He brushed her hands away, trying to regain some of his control, and she didn't protest. She merely picked up the condom packet and opened it for him, getting out the condom and holding it ready in her hand, looking at him.

Her misty grey gaze felt like cool rain on his overheated skin, and for some reason he suddenly felt outside himself with desperation.

'Do you want me to—?' she began.

'No,' he interrupted roughly, grabbing the condom from her and rolling it down in a fast, efficient movement to hide the slight shake of his hands. 'This is part of your punishment, *cara*. You don't get to touch me whenever you want.'

Her head fell back slightly as he reached for her again, pulling her once more to the edge of the desk, and she looked up at him from beneath her lashes, her gaze silvery. There was that thing again, that gentleness, that warmth. The understanding that he hadn't asked for and didn't know what to do with.

'But you can touch me,' she said softly. 'You can touch me whenever you want. I won't ever stop you.'

'Then you're a fool,' he said roughly, not sure why those words made him feel so angry or so desperate. 'You give a man like me an inch and I'll take a mile, don't you know that?' Because he would. His mother had hated that about him, how he'd kept pushing in a constant effort to make her feel better, to make everything okay, when all she'd wanted was to be left alone. Greedy, that was what he was, and selfish too.

This he already knew and accepted about himself. And he owned it.

'Yes.' She lifted her hands to his chest, stroking him gently through the cotton of his shirt as if he was a wild beast that she needed to soothe. 'But perhaps a man like you needs to figure out why he wants to take that mile.' Her gaze was full of something he couldn't interpret. 'Especially when I can just give it to you.'

No, he didn't want her surrender. He didn't want her gentleness. He didn't want that soft look or that warmth. No one had ever just given themselves to him like that, and why that felt wrong, he didn't know. But he'd let it consume him four years ago and he wasn't going to let it do the same thing again.

So he didn't say anything. Instead he put one hand on her thigh and gripped her tightly, then he took himself in the other and pushed inside her.

Hard.

She gave a soft gasp, her body jerking against his, the slick heat of her making it impossible to think. Impossible even to breathe. Her muscles had clamped tightly around him and there was a moment where all he could think about was the first time he'd had her, against the wall of the villa on that island, and he hadn't been able to believe the intensity of the pleasure that had hit him.

He still couldn't believe it.

Her fingers curled into his shirt, holding on tight, but beneath the glaze of heat in her eyes he could still see that strangely understanding look.

As if she knew exactly what he was trying to do.

'Summer,' he said, the name she'd given him on the island slipping out before he could stop it.

And her hands slid up his chest, her arms twining around his neck, a sigh escaping her at the sound of that name. Her eyes were full of heat and something else he couldn't read.

He couldn't look away. Putting his hand at the small of her back, he held her tight against him as he drew himself out of her then pushed back in. Slower this time, drawing out the sensation.

'Oh...' Matilda arched her back, pressing her soft, full breasts against him, looking up at him with so much heat and wonder, he could hardly breathe.

Because he felt it too, that intense pleasure and deep sense of connection they'd both experienced back on the island. It was still there and it was still strong.

'Summer,' he murmured again, rougher, unable to help himself, watching sensation unfurl in her eyes.

'Oh...*yes*...' she whispered. 'Enzo...'

Pleasure uncurled down his spine in a hot, slow lick. And suddenly he was ravenous, desperate. Her hands were smoothing over his shoulders beneath his jacket, finding the collar of his shirt and pushing underneath it, searching for his skin, and he growled, his control slowly slipping out of his grip.

He tried to hold onto it, cupping the soft curve of her delicious butt, squeezing her to keep her still as he drew himself out then slid back in, deeper, harder.

Except her thighs clenched around his waist and she groaned, rocking her hips against his, her fingers fumbling with his tie and the buttons of his shirt as she tried to get them undone.

She was so tight and wet. So hot.

And abruptly the last of his control was gone.

He buried one hand in her hair again, the silkiness of it sliding against his skin, and tugged her head back once more. Then he kissed her passionately, savagely, bending her back on the desk and thrusting inside her, something inside him howling for more.

She put her arms around him and held onto him tightly, giving him everything as she lifted her hips to his, panting his name over and over.

'You'll never get this from anyone else, *cara*,' he growled against her mouth, barely aware of what he was saying. 'Only me.' He slammed into her, making her gasp. 'Only ever me.' Another hard thrust. 'Tell me you understand.'

'I do.' Her voice sounded cracked. 'I understand. Oh, Enzo…*please*…'

He wanted to keep it going to draw it out even longer, but he was at the end. So he took his hand from her back and slipped it between their heated bodies, stroking over the sensitive bud between her thighs, pressing down as he moved. She shivered and cried out, pressing her face against his neck, her inner muscles clenching hard around him.

Finally he let himself go, one hand gripping her hair, drowning himself in the sweetness of her mouth and the heat of her body, slamming himself inside her until the pleasure exploded in his head like a bomb.

Then he gripped her as the climax broke over him, holding her tight.

Because she wasn't going to leave him. Not again. Not ever again.

He would make sure of it.

CHAPTER NINE

A WEEK LATER Matilda stared at herself in the mirror of Enzo's bedroom.

A woman dressed all in silver stared back, glittering from the soles of her feet to the top of her head.

The gown Enzo had bought for her to wear to the engagement party he'd arranged was a work of art. She would have been happy to choose one for herself, but he'd insisted, and since she hadn't felt that strongly about it she'd let him have his way.

She turned in the mirror slightly, watching the light move over the silver sequins that were sewn into the bodice of the gown. The sequins were thick down to the waist and then became sparser, sparkling here and there on the skirt like a scattering of diamonds. It made her look as if she'd stepped out from under a shower of stardust.

The neckline was deep—almost to her belly button—and there was a long tulle underskirt that swirled around her. The neckline and fitted shape of the bodice drew attention to the lush curves of her breasts and hips, making the most of her classic hourglass figure.

She'd never had a gown before, not like this. It was beautiful. And the way the hairstylist who Enzo had called in had done her hair—pulled back into a gleaming red chignon—made her look…well… *She* was beautiful too.

But she didn't feel like herself, and she wasn't quite sure why, as she'd been totally on board with the engagement party idea itself.

She and Enzo had decided that a party was the best way both to announce their engagement and to introduce Simon to the world as their son. Then afterwards a big wedding would distract anyone from asking questions about where Simon had been for the first four years of his life.

Matilda had been expecting the discussion about what they'd tell the press to be a difficult one, but either Enzo wasn't angry at her about it any more, or he'd somehow locked it down, because he was very calm about it.

They'd eventually decided that their story would be that they'd kept Simon's existence out of the headlines deliberately to keep attention away from him.

Enzo seemed to be sure they could keep gossip to a minimum so she'd let him handle it. Their relationship might be problematic, but she knew that he cared very much about Simon's wellbeing and would do his utmost to protect it.

Simon himself had been ecstatic when they'd both

told him together that his mother would be marrying his papa.

The excitement on his face had made a bittersweet feeling twist through her: regret that her fear had ended up denying her son a family right from the start and a kind of relief that she could give it to him now.

But at what cost to you?

She stared at herself in the mirror again, a woman she didn't recognise.

There was no cost, though, was there? She would never have to worry about money or about whether not having a father was doing her son harm. She would have a gorgeous husband and all the physical passion she could ever want. She would be wanted. She would belong somewhere and to someone.

But...

Matilda shut the thought down firmly as she sensed movement behind her.

She didn't turn around—she could see who it was in the reflection of the mirror.

Enzo.

He was dressed in a tux for the evening and the austere black suited him, the cut outlining his powerful shoulders and lean hips, while the colour made his black hair gleam and highlighted the brilliant gold of his eyes.

Her heartbeat sped up the way it always did whenever he came near her, and she had to moisten her suddenly dry mouth.

His smile was satisfied and hot as he came up behind her, staring at her in the mirror as his hands settled possessively on her waist. 'Yes,' he murmured. 'I knew that would look beautiful on you.'

Her chest hurt for some reason. The way he looked at her, the way he held her, made everything inside her tighten with instinctive yearning.

It was difficult to fight the longing inside her that had somehow grown worse since she'd come to Italy, the need to belong somewhere and to someone. Because she hadn't really had either of those things, not since her parents had died.

And it was hard being with Enzo. Hard when every time he looked at her, every time he touched her, it was with possession. Except she knew it wasn't really *her* that he was possessive about. He wanted her body and their intense physical chemistry, and the fact that she was Simon's mother. But she was acutely aware that he wouldn't be marrying her if she hadn't pushed him into it.

The knowledge sat inside her like a small splinter of glass.

'It's lovely,' she said, trying not to think about it now.

Enzo's gaze met hers in the mirror. 'I can hear a "but".'

Of course he could. He was so irritatingly perceptive about some things, annoyingly dense about others.

Maybe today he could have the truth.

'I feel…strange in it.'

One dark brow rose in surprise. 'Why?'

'It's very…grand. I feel a bit like an imposter, to be honest.'

His hands tightened on her waist. 'You're not an imposter, Matilda. You're my fiancée. And as for the dress being grand, yes, it is. If I still had my kingdom, you would be my queen.'

They'd never discussed his royal past. He'd mentioned it back on the island and she'd been fascinated and full of questions. But she'd sensed that the subject was a painful one and, because she'd also been too unsure of herself around him then, she hadn't pressed.

But now… Well, those questions were still there. And maybe she should ask them. She didn't want to marry a man she didn't really know, after all.

'I remember you telling me about that,' she said. 'You never said how you lost it, though.'

'I didn't lose it.' A sharp edge had crept into his voice. 'That was my father's doing. He didn't care about the country he was supposed to protect or his subjects. He just wanted power. He made one mistake too many and the government decided they'd had enough and got rid of him. And his family too.'

She studied him in the mirror, watching his expression. 'What happened?'

'We were told to leave.' The aristocratic lines of Enzo's face hardened. 'Soldiers came one night and ordered us off the island. We only had a couple of hours to collect our belongings before we were put in a boat to the mainland.'

Her heart clenched unexpectedly hard. She knew

what it was like to have life change suddenly. To have to pack up your things and go somewhere else, with no idea what it would be like when you got there. That was what she'd had to do when her parents had died.

Was that where his anger came from? Because she'd sensed it the day he'd taken her on his desk and had wondered if it had deeper roots than simply anger with her and what she'd done. She'd even asked him, but he'd never answered her question.

She searched his face. Yes, of course he was angry about leaving his home all those years ago. That was why he was so single-mindedly pursuing this idea of building a home and a family on the damn island he'd bought from Henry, wasn't it?

No wonder he thought of her as his queen. He was trying to rebuild his kingdom.

'That must have been hard,' she said quietly. 'You were only fifteen, weren't you?'

'Yes.' Something glittered in his gaze and it was definitely anger. 'Old enough to realise what was happening. And what I was losing.'

Losing a home. Yes, God, she knew what that was like.

'I was ten when my parents died,' she said, wanting to offer him a little something of herself in return. 'And then I was shipped off to my mother's sister to live. My aunt and uncle were childless, and really didn't want me, but they took me in anyway because there was no one else. So, I know what it's like to lose the life you thought you'd have. It's really, really hard.'

His gaze was sharp as it met hers in the mirror. 'You never told me that you'd lost your parents.'

Had she not? Perhaps she hadn't. When they'd talked to each other, they'd only spoken about the future and what they wanted from it, not about the past. Or at least, she hadn't.

'Well,' she said, 'it's not a particularly happy story so you didn't miss anything.'

'Tell me.'

That sharp expression gleamed in his eyes and the inevitable longing rose because she did want to tell him. She wanted to share herself with him. But along with it came a feeling of vulnerability, as if she'd just revealed a weakness to him.

'You tell me about your family first,' she said, prevaricating. 'You know more about me than I do about you.'

He'd tensed behind her, his posture stiff. 'Yes, you do.'

'No.' She stared at him in the mirror. 'All you told me was that you wanted a home because you'd lost yours. And that one day you wanted a family as well. You didn't tell me anything else beyond that.'

A muscle flicked in his jaw, his fingers tight on her waist. But then he said, 'There's nothing more to add. My father was a power-hungry, bitter bastard who didn't know how to be a man, let alone a king, and my mother put up with his rages like a martyr.'

She stared at him, watching the anger he couldn't quite hide smoulder like coals in his eyes.

'We had nothing when we came off that boat,' he

went on. 'Less than nothing. Luca was more interested in making useless plans for trying to get his
throne back than actually being a husband and father,
and my mother cared more about her own unhappiness than she did about anything else. She left in the
end and took Dante with her. I had to stay with him.'
Bitterness laced his tone. 'He didn't care, not about
my mother leaving or about the fact that I stayed.
All that mattered to him was power and he couldn't
reconcile himself to having none.'

Her heart clenched. Her father in her memory had
been loving and warm, which had made the loss of
him and her mother so much harder. But at least she'd
had them and at least they had loved her.

Had Enzo had anyone who'd cared?

'I'm sorry,' she said, knowing it sounded ineffec-
tual and useless, but not knowing what else to offer
him. 'He sounds awful. And your mother leaving…
You kind of lost both parents, didn't you?'

The glittering look in his eyes focused on her all
of a sudden. 'Yes. I did. Tell me about yours.'

Her heart clenched a little tighter. 'There's nothing much to tell. But they loved me and I loved them.
They died in a car accident on the way to pick me
up from school.'

Slowly Enzo's hands slid around her waist, his
palms coming to rest possessively against her stomach. His body was at her back, a hot, hard wall of
strength she could lean against if she wanted to,
and there was something inexplicably reassuring
about that.

'And how did you end up marrying St George?' There was a thread of warning in his voice, a protective anger. 'To get away from your aunt and uncle?'

'No. They…weren't very demonstrative or loving, but they weren't unkind to me. They gave me a roof over my head and paid for my schooling. They brought me up.' She didn't want him thinking that they'd been awful to her, because they hadn't been. 'And I married Henry because they didn't have much money and were going to lose their house. Henry was a family friend. He said he'd give them the money if I married him.'

Enzo frowned. 'Why didn't he just give them the money—without the marriage?'

'Because he was lonely and wanted a companion. And he didn't want the gossip that would come from a young woman living with a much older man.' She paused. 'I think he knew that I didn't want to do it, so he made sure to attach a few strings.'

Enzo's frown turned into a scowl. 'He manipulated you, in other words.'

A defensive anger on Henry's behalf rose because, no, the initial thought of the marriage hadn't been ideal, but he hadn't been awful to her and, after all, she'd agreed to it. 'Well, I didn't want to marry him initially. But the money he was going to give my aunt and uncle would help them. And they'd done so much for me—'

'Done so much for you?' Enzo interrupted harshly. 'They took you in as a family is supposed to with an orphaned child. You don't owe them anything. It's not your fault you lost your parents.'

Matilda felt herself flush. 'I know that.' Because of course she did. 'But they didn't have a lot of money and my schooling was very expensive. It didn't seem like a big thing to do.'

But there was a gleaming edge in his eyes, a scalpel cutting away the protective layers she'd placed around her soul. 'Why are you defending them?'

'Why do you care that I am?' she shot back before she could help herself.

A tense, thick silence fell.

His gaze burned into hers, the muscle in the side of his jaw leaping.

God, why had she said that? She didn't want to fight with him, not again.

She put her hands over his where they rested against her abdomen, wanting to push him away, uncomfortable all of a sudden, but it was like pushing stone. He didn't move.

'That's why you were so upset when St George let you go, wasn't it?' he said, ignoring her question. 'Because you cared about him. And you wanted him to care about you. You wanted your aunt and uncle to care too.'

A helpless pain twisted inside her. Of course Enzo had seen her reaction to the way Henry had let her go. He wasn't a stupid man; he'd make the connection.

She looked away from him, unable to bear his gaze any longer. Afraid he might see that longing she'd tried to hide. That longing for a place to be and someone to be with. To be more than just a thing that no one wanted, or passed on when her usefulness had come to an end.

'Matilda,' he said softly. 'Look at me.'

She didn't want to. She couldn't bear him knowing what was inside her. It shouldn't matter to her that he knew, but he was right, she did care. And she didn't want to.

One of his hands moved, rising to grip her chin and lift her head, forcing her to meet his sharp, golden stare in the mirror.

She trembled, feeling like she was being cut to shreds.

'Tell me what you're afraid of,' he ordered, the words an irresistible command.

There was no point trying to hide from him; there never had been. He saw everything.

But she didn't want to give him the satisfaction of knowing he'd dragged it from her so she straightened against him. Met his gaze. 'I'm afraid of not belonging anywhere.' She flung the truth at him like a challenge. 'Of not belonging to anyone. Of being just a thing that no one wanted to start with, or passed on to someone else when they lose interest.' Her throat felt tight and she was trembling, but adrenaline was firing through her and now she'd started she felt as though she couldn't stop. 'I'm afraid of rocking the boat. Of putting a foot out of line. I'm afraid to disagree or protest, or even just voice an opinion. Because I know what will happen if I do.' She stared right into his eyes, daring him to agree. 'I'll be got rid of as if I was nothing. Less than nothing.'

She didn't know what she expected, though there was a part of her that was terrified he'd sneer at her, or laugh and tell her she was being foolish.

But he did neither of those things.

There was a flame in his eyes, bright and hot, and burning hotter as she looked at him. Then suddenly he spun her round so she was facing him, the intensity in his expression burning her to the ground.

'You're not nothing,' he said roughly. 'And you're not a thing. When I said for ever, Matilda, I meant it. You belong with me. I will never get rid of you. You're mine.' And then before she could say a word he lowered his head and took her mouth as if he owned it.

They'd made love many times in the days since he'd taken her on the desk in his office. But he'd always been very deliberate about it. Very measured.

He was not measured now.

He pushed her up against the mirror at her back, kissing her harder, deeper, nipping her bottom lip, sending tiny darts of pain through her.

His. She was his. He would never let her go.

She was shaking and she found she'd threaded her fingers through his black hair, holding on tight to him as he pressed her against the cold mirror, his body covering hers.

'It's not about me, though, is it?' Her voice was husky against his marauding mouth and she didn't even know why she was saying it. A dare, perhaps.

Certainly a challenge, as she'd never been able to resist challenging him. 'You want a kingdom. You want a queen. You don't want me.'

'Don't tell me what I do or do not want.' He nipped her again, hard, making her gasp. Then he lowered his head further, his teeth against her neck. 'If a queen was all that I wanted, I could marry anyone. But I'm not. I'm going to marry you.'

'For Simon's sake.'

'No, not only for Simon's sake.' He lifted his head, put one hand on either side of her head on the mirror behind them then stared down at her, letting her see what was blazing in his eyes. 'I want you, Matilda.'

She couldn't stop trembling, her body coming helplessly alive under the touch of his mouth and the fierce, demanding heat of him. 'You want me in your bed, Enzo. That's all.'

'Yes. I do.' He shifted his hands, cupping her face between them. 'But there's nothing "all" about that. I could have anyone in my bed, *cara*, but the only woman I want there is you.'

It wasn't exactly what she wanted to hear, but it was enough. Enough to push the doubts away, to heal a little piece of her wounded heart.

And, as she was good at taking what she could when she could get it, she took what she could now, curling her fingers tighter in his hair and pulling his mouth down on hers.

She didn't want to think about the rest of her heart, the parts that wouldn't heal and that he wouldn't be able to fix. And most especially she didn't want to think about the fact that she wanted him to be the one to fix them.

Instead, she thought about his teeth nipping at her neck and his hands stroking the curve of her breasts through the fabric of her silver gown, his thumbs circling her aching nipples, making them hard.

'The party,' she panted, arching into his hands.

'Damn the party.' His voice was a growl. 'Rock the boat, *cara*. Put a foot out of line. Tell me your opinion. Now.'

But she couldn't tell him what she really wanted, not when she was afraid to articulate it even to herself.

She could rock the boat a little, though. She could rock *his* boat.

'Give me room,' Matilda whispered, then pushed gently at him, making him release her and take a step back.

Then she dropped to her knees in front of him.

He didn't try to stop her as she reached for his belt and undid it, or make a move as she opened his trousers and pulled down the zip. He only murmured his approval as she reached into his boxers and curled her fingers around his hard, thick length.

Then he leaned forward as she drew him out and put his hands on the glass of the mirror again, looking down at her with that compelling amber gaze gone smoky and lambent with desire.

'I tried to forget you, Matilda,' he said unexpectedly, his voice husky. 'For four years I tried, but I couldn't do it. And I was angry at you for that. But you're here, and you're mine, and you're what I want, understand?'

She did. And she also understood that he was giving her what he could; that, although he hadn't said it straight out, he did care.

Pity it's not enough.

But it was enough for her now, though, and she took it, holding his gaze as she guided him to her lips, as she touched her tongue to the head of his shaft. As she licked him the way she remembered him having taught her, watching the flames ignite in his eyes.

And then she took him all the way into her mouth, losing herself in the salty, rich taste of him and the silky texture of his skin. He made a deep, rough sound as she did so, the desire in his eyes burning her through.

Yes, this was enough. Being the one he wanted. The only one he wanted.

She tightened her grip on him and began to suck, watching as the muscles in his neck and jaw grew tight, a soundless snarl twisting his lips, deciding that four years wasn't going to be enough. She was going to burn herself into his brain so completely that he'd *never* forget her.

So she teased him and taunted him, using her mouth and her tongue, loving the sounds that she drew from him. And when he reached down eventually and thrust one hand into her elegant hairstyle, making it fall apart into long curls that fell over her shoulders, she ignored his powerful grip. She kept up her rhythm until he was growling in rough, savage Italian, his hips moving in time with the pull of her mouth.

He was near the edge and she wanted to keep him there as long as possible. But at the last minute he took control, shoving his other hand in her hair and totally ruining what was left of her hairstyle as he thrust into her mouth.

She didn't care by then, though, gripping his thighs as he threw back his head, making him roar her name as the climax hit him.

Afterwards she had to lean forward and rest her head on his rock-hard abdomen, her heart beating like a drum in her ears, the pulse between her legs feeling almost as loud.

He moved his hands lazily in her hair, seemingly not caring about her sleek hairstyle any longer, twining his fingers in her curls then moving down to caress her neck. Despite herself, a deep sense of satisfaction crept through her.

Yes, she could do this. She could.

'Up,' he murmured, his voice rough and lazy.

Slowly, she rose to her feet.

A very male, very territorial look gleamed in his eyes that had her pulse beating faster, harder.

He pushed her gently back against the mirror and took her mouth again, kissing her very thoroughly, as if he enjoyed the taste of himself on her. She let him, winding her arms around his neck, relaxing against him. Enjoying his heat and the possessive way he held her.

Then he pulled back, giving her a sharp, intense look as he tucked himself away and righted his clothes. 'I need to return the favour, but unfortunately there is a party we need to get to.'

She shivered, aware of the pulsing ache between her thighs and of how much she wanted him to touch her. But he was right; the party couldn't wait.

'Hold that thought,' she murmured.

There was obvious reluctance in his eyes, which gave her a small warm glow, then he reached into the pocket of his trousers. 'Before I forget, I have something for you.'

All thoughts of being touched vanished from Matilda's head as he brought out a small black box and held it out to her. 'What's this?'

'Open it and see.' His expression was fierce.

Her heart beating a little too fast, she reached out and took the box, flipping it open.

Inside, a ring gleamed. A jewel of glittering gold surrounded by what looked like diamonds and set in a band of silver. It was heavy, medieval-looking, and she had the sense that it was very, very old.

It was beautiful, the stone the exact colour of his eyes.

She touched the jewel, the facets glittering in the light of the bedroom. 'Enzo...' she breathed helplessly. 'This is amazing.'

'It's the royal ring of Monte Santa Maria.' He took the box from her and extracted the ring. 'The stone is a yellow diamond and very rare. The colour is to signify the golden eyes of the Cardinali line.' He

reached for her left hand and took it in his, looking at her with those very same royal eyes. 'Every
king wore it. And now my queen will wear it.' And
he gently pushed the ring onto her wedding finger.

Despite its size and weight, it fit her perfectly.

There was an ache in her chest and in the back of
her throat. Henry had given her an engagement ring
too, a pretty diamond. But she'd never worn it and
had never really thought about why.

She knew why now, though. Because it hadn't
meant anything to either of them. The ring had been
a signifier of a promise, but not a promise of love.

It had been a signifier of duty. Her duty.

*Don't get excited. This ring doesn't signify love
either.*

No, it didn't. But once again Enzo had given her
something. And this particular something was important to him.

She met his fierce golden stare and held it. 'I love
it. And I'll wear it with pride.'

He didn't smile this time, that fierce look only becoming more intense. 'You're mine now, Matilda,' he
said, and this time she felt the weight in the words,
heavy and certain, like a vow. 'Let's go and tell the
world.'

CHAPTER TEN

THE BALLROOM OF the villa was full of the cream of Milanese high society, as well as famous faces from other parts of the world: a couple of film stars—even though Enzo found actors frivolous—a politician or two, heads of various industries, plus all the members of Italy's aristocratic families he could find.

No one had refused his invitation. Everyone wanted to know who'd finally caught Enzo Cardinali's eye. He'd allowed a rumour of scandal to filter through to the media to generate a bit of interest; he could hardly hide the fact that his new fiancée had very recently been Henry St George's wife, after all.

But his hopes that that particular scandal would be forgotten when people found out about his son seemed to hold true.

Simon held court in the room full of people like the future king he should have been.

Enzo introduced Simon around himself, holding the boy's hand while he did so, paying attention to his son's responses, watching for signs that Simon was uncomfortable or tired.

He'd told the boy earlier that they were having a special party so people could meet him and that greeting people politely was what a host did. It might be boring, but saying hello was a good thing to do, and afterwards he could go and play if he wanted.

But Enzo needn't have worried. Simon liked people a lot and took his duties as host very seriously. Only his grip on Enzo's hand betrayed a slight nervousness as he greeted his guests solemnly and thanked them all for coming.

Everyone in the entire room was charmed.

Certainly they seemed more interested in the little boy than the woman who gripped Enzo's arm as he moved around the room, the ring he'd given her flashing on her finger.

And he found he didn't mind that.

He felt even more hungry and possessive after what had happened between them upstairs; after she'd told him of her fears, revealed her vulnerabilities to him then had gone down on her knees and proceeded to show him exactly why he'd never been able to forget her for all those years.

He supposed he shouldn't have let himself care so much about her fears, but he'd hated the thought of her being afraid she wasn't wanted. That she didn't belong anywhere or to anyone.

And he'd been furious on her behalf at her aunt and uncle, and at damn St George, for making her feel that way.

She was his now; he'd claimed her. She belonged to him. And he would protect her in a way her own

blood relations and the people who were supposed
to care for her hadn't.

Careful. She's starting to matter to you.

A certain unease shifted inside him. Well, and
what if she did start to matter to him? She needed to
matter to someone and that someone could be him.
For his son's sake, of course, but also for his own.
He didn't want her to be unhappy in this marriage,
didn't want her to lose any of her passion.

*She needs more than that. She needs more than
you're willing to give and you know it.*

The unease deepened, though he tried to ignore it.

What more could she need anyway? He would
give her a home and the weight of all his power
and money behind her to help her do whatever she
wanted. Finish her degree, carve a career for herself if she chose. And then there was the physical
pleasure he could give her. What more, apart from
that, was there?

He'd tried more to keep his mother happy, to keep
her from drinking, to keep her from leaving, but
it hadn't been enough. 'What is there to stay for?'
she'd spat at him just before she'd walked out the
door. 'Your father will only be happy with a throne,
and as for you, well, it's not my happiness you care
about, but your own. You're selfish, just like him.'

No, it wasn't he who was selfish. It was them.
They were the selfish ones. It was true that his father
only cared about power, but his mother had her own
streak of selfishness too. She'd only been interested
in her own misery, not anyone else's.

Certainly not his.

His father only wanted more power and his mother had wanted him to be someone else.

Neither of them had wanted him.

A couple of important politicians smiled at Matilda as Simon made his greeting, one of them leaning in and murmuring something to her about his own son who was the same age.

She smiled back and nodded, her face bright, touching Simon's head lightly as she murmured something in return that made the politician laugh.

Well, it was too bad if she wanted more. He'd taken a leaf out of his mother's book. He had nothing more to give.

The thought made Enzo's chest ache, and he wasn't sure why, so he ignored it.

Not long after that, there was a fuss near the door to the ballroom.

It was Dante arriving—late, as per usual—so Enzo took both his son and his new fiancée over to meet him.

'This is your uncle Dante,' he said to Simon. 'Say hello.'

Simon did so—in perfect Italian as Enzo had been teaching him—then frowned at Dante before looking up at Enzo. 'Do I have to like him?'

Dante blinked while Enzo tried not to smile. 'No. But he'll be your uncle all the same.'

'You can act as if you like him,' Matilda offered generously, smiling. 'That's the polite thing to do.'

'It's fine.' Dante grinned down at his nephew.

'You don't even have to be polite to me. I'm not polite to anyone else.'

Simon's eyes went wide. 'Really?'

At that, Enzo decided that one minute of Dante's company was one minute too many and leaned down to whisper to Simon to go and find Maria, as it was nearly bed time.

The boy pulled a face but raced off to find the housekeeper.

When Enzo straightened up, he found his brother surveying Matilda, a certain appreciative gleam in his eye.

It made something inside him growl.

He stepped closer to her and put an arm around her waist, drawing her close. 'And this is your sister-in-law-to-be,' he said, putting emphasis on the 'sister-in-law' part of the sentence. 'Matilda St George. Matilda, this is my terrible brother, Dante Cardinali.'

Dante gave him an amused glance. 'Calm down, Enzo. I'm not going to steal her from you.' He held out a hand. 'Delighted to meet you, Matilda.'

But Enzo did not feel particularly calm. The sight of Matilda's fingers in Dante's big, tanned palm made him want to bare his teeth. Which was ridiculous. Dante was his brother. He wouldn't do anything to take Matilda from him.

Matilda smiled at Dante, as bright and as beautiful with him as she'd been with everyone else. 'Nice to meet you too.'

She was so lovely, her smile warm and generous. *She doesn't smile that way with you.*

'I like your ring,' Dante observed, looking down at the Cardinali royal signet ring. 'Looks familiar.'

'It's from my safe,' Enzo said, far more frigidly than he'd intended to, trying to ignore the persistent ache in his chest and the insidious thought in his head. 'I had it resized for her. You have a problem with her wearing it?'

Dante smiled, but his dark eyes were uncomfortably sharp, as if he knew exactly what was going on in Enzo's head. 'Of course not. You didn't want it for yourself?'

'Why would I?' Enzo couldn't quite temper his tone. 'It's a king's ring and I'm not a king.'

A silence fell, his sharp words echoing oddly in it, both Matilda and Dante staring at him: Dante with that knowing look while Matilda's eyes held nothing but concern.

Dio, what was wrong with him?

He cast around for something to say that would smooth over the moment, but that wasn't his forte and his brother got in first instead, asking Matilda some innocuous question. A minute or so later the pair of them were chatting like old friends, Matilda laughing at something Dante said.

She doesn't laugh that way with you either.

No, he didn't make her laugh. He'd never been able to make his mother laugh either. Then again, how important was laughter when he could make her scream with pleasure instead? Surely that was all she needed?

Yet the ache in his chest grew deeper, wider, and

he wanted to tighten his arm around her, pull her out of this crowded ballroom and go somewhere quiet where he could make her scream again for him. Ease that damn ache that wouldn't go away.

But he didn't. He wasn't going to let himself give into it. But he did need to get a handle on himself. Perhaps he should go and check on Simon. Seeing his son always made him feel better.

Matilda had put her hand on his arm, but the touch was more than he could bear just now, so calmly he removed his arm from underneath her hand. 'Excuse me, *cara*. I just need to go and see where our son went.'

Then, without waiting for her to reply, Enzo turned and strode out of the room.

Much later, Matilda stood in the corner of the crowded ballroom, surveying all the people, searching for a tall, dark figure and not seeing it.

Something was wrong. She'd known it the moment she'd stepped into the ballroom with Enzo and felt the tension begin to gather in him, getting tighter and tighter as time had gone on.

She'd tried to ignore it, told herself that whatever was bothering him she'd ask him about it later, but then he'd suddenly excused himself on the pretext of looking for Simon and he hadn't come back.

Was it her? Something she'd done? Something to do with what had happened between them upstairs? Had he decided he didn't want her to be his after all?

'You're looking pale,' her ridiculously handsome

brother-in-law said, coming to stand beside her. 'Is everything okay?'

And that was another strange thing, the icy waves that had poured off Enzo the moment his brother had taken her hand. If she hadn't thought better she would have said that he was jealous. Which was odd, because what did he have to be jealous of?

She liked Dante and, yes, he was gorgeous, but she didn't want him. He didn't look at her the way Enzo did, as if he wanted to eat her alive, the fire of his ferocious soul burning in his eyes. Dante was all lazy, sensual charm, while Enzo was all demand, all possessive heat. She liked that.

No, she loved it.

You love him.

Ice water trickled down her back. Insanity. She didn't love Enzo. How could she? She barely knew him.

'I'm fine thank you.' She put down the wine glass she'd been carrying, though she'd drunk nothing from it. 'I was just wondering where Enzo had got to.'

Dante gave her a reassuring smile. 'Don't children get fractious around bedtimes? Perhaps my nephew is giving him a run for his money.'

'He might. But Simon's always very good about bedtimes when Enzo's around.' A nervous feeling sat in her gut. 'Maybe you're right, though. Maybe I should go and find him.'

'Matilda,' Dante said quietly. 'Be careful of Enzo.'

She stilled and looked at him in shock. 'Be careful? What are you talking about?

Dante's dark eyes were very direct. 'He's a man who's lost a great many things. Things he's been trying for years to get back.'

'Yes, I do know that.'

'Our mother left not long after we were exiled,' Dante went on in a low voice. 'And she took me with her, leaving Enzo with our father. He never speaks about the years he spent with Dad, but Luca Cardinali wasn't an easy man to live with. And, after he died, Enzo was alone for a long time.'

Something shifted inside her, a tight, hot feeling. She remembered the bitterness lacing his voice as he'd told her about his parents, the heat of anger running like a current underneath it.

She'd asked him weeks ago what he had to be angry about and, well, maybe the roots of it lay there. In his past.

'That sounds awful.' Her voice was thick but she didn't bother trying to hide it.

Dante's gaze was as sharp as his brother's all of a sudden. 'You care for him, don't you?'

It's more than care. You love him. You've been in love with him ever since you met him. That's why you ran from him.

The ballroom blurred in her vision, her eyes suddenly full of tears, her chest hollow. She didn't want to be in love with Enzo Cardinali. He wanted her, and he'd told her he was going to keep her for ever, and that would be enough for her. Carefully, she hadn't thought about that doubt tugging at her. She'd pushed it aside and told herself that belonging to someone was all she'd wanted.

But it won't be.

'Yes,' she said, her voice hoarse. 'I do care.' Because it was true and, even though she wanted to keep on denying it, she couldn't any longer.

And maybe Dante saw it, because something in his eyes softened. 'Good. Because he's not an easy man to care for and he needs someone strong.'

Someone strong. Was that her?

She wanted to ask him more questions, but someone caught Dante's arm and he was led into a conversation with some other people, leaving Matilda on her own.

Her heart felt sore, as if someone had stepped on it.

Enzo, left all alone by his mother to his power-hungry father. Neither of them had cared about him, that was the subtext, wasn't it? His father had wanted a throne more than a son, and his mother had simply…abandoned him.

His family had fractured completely. Like hers.

Suddenly all she wanted was to find him, to see what was wrong, whether he was all right, so she shoved aside thoughts of love and gave the ballroom another search. But he definitely wasn't there so she slipped out and went upstairs to Simon's bedroom.

But her son was already in bed, sleeping soundly, no sign of Enzo.

He wasn't anywhere in the upper levels of the

villa, so she came back down and searched the lower floor.

She didn't see any sign of him until she pushed open the door to the library and there he was, standing beside the fireplace, one hand on the mantelpiece, the other in his pocket, looking down at the unlit grate.

The expression on his beautiful, fierce face was unreadable, but there was something about it that made her aching heart tighten even further.

'What do you want, Matilda?' He didn't look round. 'Simon is in bed.'

'I know. I just saw him.' She closed the door quietly and came over to where he stood. 'I only wanted to find out where you'd gone. You left rather suddenly and—'

'I'm fine.' The words were flat. 'I only needed a couple of moments to myself. Go back to the party.'

She should. But of course she didn't.

Dante had told her that he'd been alone for a long time, that he needed someone. And she knew what loneliness felt like; she felt it every day. She could be that someone that he needed, couldn't she?

He wanted her after all, had told her that she belonged to him. So why not? After all, he'd given her something she'd needed herself up there in that bedroom, so maybe it was time for her to return the favour.

Matilda didn't move. 'What's going on, Enzo?'

'There's nothing going on.'

'Yes, there is. You were standing in the ballroom

glaring around and looking like you wanted to chew through concrete.'

There was a brief silence.

He turned his head and looked at her, golden eyes icy, a wall behind them. 'And?'

She ignored the cold note in his voice. 'You were giving a very good impression of jealousy back there. In fact, you looked like you wanted to kill your brother. Is that the issue?'

'I wasn't jealous.' His voice didn't change. It was cold, hard. 'Was there something important you wanted to talk to me about, Matilda? We have guests, don't forget.'

But she knew what he was doing: he was shutting her out, putting some distance between them. The idiot. He wouldn't let her do this to him, so why did he think she'd let him do it to her?

She closed the distance between them, coming to where he stood, looking up into his icy, golden gaze. 'Is it me?' she asked bluntly. 'Did I do something?'

'No, of course not. Why would you think that?'

'Because something's wrong, and you're not telling me what it is, so why wouldn't I think that?'

The expression on his face shut down. 'Go back to the party, Matilda.'

He was so tall standing there in front of the fireplace, dark and stern in his black suit. Austere and beautiful too. Of the lazy heat she'd seen burning in his eyes upstairs in the bedroom, there was no sign.

There was nothing but cold there now.

Determination settled down inside her. Well, she

wasn't going to let him freeze her out. She was his. She belonged to him. He'd put that ring on her finger upstairs and that meant something.

He needed someone. She would be that someone.

Matilda lifted a hand to his face, half-expecting his skin to be cold, considering the chill radiating off him. But it wasn't. When she laid her fingers against his sharp jaw, the heat of his skin just about seared her fingertips.

He didn't move, but a muscle leapt under her touch. 'What are you doing?' His voice remained frigid yet she could see some of that familiar heat beginning to glow in his eyes. 'Go back to the party.'

'No.' She pressed her fingers against his hard jawline. 'Not until you tell me what's going on.'

He stayed very still, the glow in his eyes beginning to get brighter, his gaze becoming more focused, more intense. And still he said nothing.

'You don't have to be jealous, Enzo.' She searched his face. 'It's not Dante's ring I'm wearing.'

'It's not Dante I'm concerned about,' he snapped, the ice in his voice finally breaking.

'Then what?'

Enzo reached up and circled her wrist with his long, strong fingers, holding her tight. His gaze was hot now, nothing cold about it, and it burned fiercely and bright. 'What do you want from me?' he asked suddenly, harshly. 'I can't make you laugh like he can. I can't make you smile like he can. I can't and I won't. But I can give you everything else.'

Matilda's breath caught at the anger in his eyes.

'I don't want anything else,' she said, even though it wasn't the truth.

'Then stop looking at me like you do,' Enzo said roughly. 'Because there's nothing more I can give you.'

There was a tense silence, electricity crackling between them, and it was as if she could feel every whorl of his fingertips pressed against her skin.

'I'm not looking at you like that.' She stared hard at him. 'All I asked was what's wrong? But someone wanted more from you, didn't they, Enzo? Who was it?'

His golden eyes pinned her to the spot, so fierce. Yet his thumb was moving unconsciously on her wrist, stroking her gently, igniting fires all over her skin, making embers she'd kept banked after their moment in the bedroom upstairs flare into need again. 'Why should I tell you?' he demanded. 'Why should I tell you anything at all?'

She met him stare for stare. 'Because I told you everything upstairs in the bedroom. And then I got down on my knees for you and gave you more.'

Enzo's gaze intensified. 'My father wanted power,' he said abruptly. 'And when I couldn't help him get it, he pretended I didn't exist. And my mother... She was so unhappy after we were exiled and nothing I did made it better. She drank. A lot. So one day I emptied all her wine out, thinking that would help.' His jaw clenched beneath her hand. 'She was furious. Told me that it wasn't her happiness that I cared about, only my own, that I was no

better than him. That I always wanted more than—'
He stopped. 'But it was them who wanted more, not
me. And I wasn't enough.'

Matilda's throat tightened, her heart feeling full
and painful inside her chest. She could hear his
anger, could hear too the pain running underneath
it.

It made her angry, because she knew what rejection felt like. The situation wasn't exactly like her
own, as her aunt and uncle hadn't wanted her at all,
but the hurt was the same.

'You're enough for me,' she said fiercely. 'You're
more than enough. I want you just the way you are.'

The gold in his eyes flamed, heat rising. 'But you
deserve better, Matilda.' His voice had gone rough.
'You deserve more than anything I can ever give
you.'

Something lurched inside her, but she ignored it,
shoving it aside as if it didn't mean anything. Because this wasn't about her.

She lifted her other hand so she cupped his face,
pressing her palms to his skin. 'You told me that I
was yours, that you would never let me go. And I
don't want you to, understand? I *want* to be yours.'

He didn't move, simply looked at her with that
intense, hungry expression.

'And you don't have to make me laugh,' she went
on, just as intense. 'You don't have to make me smile.
Just give me what you can and that will be enough.'
She stroked her thumbs along the tight line of his
jaw. 'It'll be more than enough.'

Enzo said nothing, but the blaze in his eyes just about burned her to the ground.

That was all the warning she got.

He bent his head and covered her mouth with his, kissing her hard and hot, with all the demand he couldn't seem to articulate.

And she met it, kissing him back, meeting him fire for fire, sliding her hands from his jaw to around his neck, arching her body against the rock-hard heat of his.

He growled, his hands on her hips, suddenly propelling her back until she was pushed up against the bookcases beside the fire, the shelves digging into her spine.

She didn't care.

She bit his lip, giving him a taste of her teeth, making him growl again, a deep, guttural sound in his throat as he pressed himself against her.

'Yes,' he murmured roughly against her mouth, his hands jerking up the skirts of her silver gown. 'This is what you need from me, *cara*.' His fingers pushed between her thighs and under the lace of her underwear, finding her slick, hot flesh, stroking her. 'This is *all* you'll ever need.'

And it was easy to believe that he was right when his fingers were touching her, sliding all around her wet sex and finding the tight little bundle of nerves where she was most sensitive, teasing it lightly.

Making her tremble, shake and shift against his hand, pleasure jolting like electricity along all her nerve endings.

And when he slid one finger inside her, tearing a groan from her throat, there was absolutely no question at all. This *was* all she ever needed.

Him. Touching her.

'Enzo…' she gasped, lifting her hips against his hand. 'More.'

He shoved her skirt up all the way, his golden eyes holding her pinned against the bookcases as much as his hot, strong body was, pulling his trousers open and freeing himself. Gripping one of her thighs, he urged her leg up and around his lean waist, and she felt herself open for him, the stretch of her muscles adding to the eroticism of the moment.

Then, still looking at her, he thrust inside her, deep and hard.

The pleasure was indescribable.

Matilda moaned, arching at the bookcases digging into her back, unable to drag her gaze away from the burning look in his beautiful face. Because, whether he knew it or not, he was demanding things from her again and this time she wanted to give them to him. She wanted to give him everything.

Because she loved him.

'Yes,' she said huskily, answering the look in his eyes, her heart full and aching. 'Take whatever you need. I'm yours, Enzo. You know that.'

And something shifted in his expression, the gold of his eyes burning impossibly brighter, like that of a predator preparing to come in for the kill.

Then he made a savage sound and jerked at her

silver gown, ripping open the delicate fabric around the neckline and baring her breasts.

She shivered as cool air moved over her skin, the feel of him inside her combining with the fierce heat of his gaze, becoming something hot, volatile. A chemistry that could explode at any moment.

He cupped one breast and she gasped at the heat of his palm against her skin, then gasped again as he dipped his head, his tongue flicking over her rapidly hardening nipple. Then he did it again and again, before sucking her nipple entirely into his mouth.

He began to thrust inside her, timing each one with the pull of his mouth on her breast, honing the pleasure into something bright and agonisingly sharp. Cutting her into shreds.

But she didn't fight it. She gave herself up to it, and to him, because that was what she'd promised him. If this was all he had to give then she would take it.

It's all you'll ever have.

Then it *was* all she'd ever have. And she was okay with that.

But she couldn't think any more as she arched in his grip, her hand lifting, pushing her fingers deep into the silk of his hair, rocking against him as he continued to suckle on her.

'Tell me this is all you want,' he demanded, his mouth brushing against her skin. 'Promise me you won't ask for anything more.'

'No,' she moaned, closing her eyes against the intensity of the pleasure. 'I won't.'

He shifted his grip then she felt him take her hand and guide it down between them, down to where they were joined. Then he placed her fingers over her own slick flesh and pressed them down. 'Say the words, Matilda.'

She shuddered as the pleasure became even sharper, even more agonising, lightning flashes behind her eyes. 'I promise I won't ask for anything more,' she said hoarsely. 'This is all I want.'

'Look at me.'

And she forced her eyes open, clashing with the brilliant gold in his.

'You'll never regret it,' he said hotly and darkly, like a vow. 'I promise you that.'

Then he pressed her fingers down and began to thrust, harder, deeper, the relentless pull of the pleasure tugging her in and dragging her under.

She closed her eyes and let herself drown in it.

And ignored the way her heart ached.

CHAPTER ELEVEN

'No,' ENZO SAID, surveying Matilda from the comfort of the plush white sofa he was sitting on. 'Not that one.'

She was standing in front of him, examining herself in the big gilt mirror leaning up against the wall of the dressing room, the wedding-dress designer kneeling at her feet and fussing with the hem of the gown she was wearing.

They were in the exclusive bridal salon that Enzo had chosen to provide a wedding gown, and he was there because he'd insisted. He wanted to look at the gowns beforehand, and he'd already refused three for various different reasons. He didn't like this one any better.

'What's wrong with it?' Matilda asked mildly, touching her hand delicately to the sleek white silk she wore.

Enzo pushed himself up from the sofa and came over to her, frowning as he examined it. 'It's too simple.' He stalked around her, taking it in from every angle. 'It's fine for an ordinary wedding, but not for ours.'

It was plain white silk with no adornments at all and it would not do. Certainly not for the kind of wedding he'd been planning.

He'd spent the past couple of weeks since their engagement party knee-deep in wedding organisation, a difficult task at such short notice, considering he wanted a big ceremony as suited the occasion.

They were to be married on his island, on the terrace, with as many important guests and attendant media as he could get his hands on.

It was, after all, a royal wedding.

And she needed a royal gown.

Matilda's lashes swept down, veiling her gaze. 'Well, if you don't like it, then of course I'll change it.'

He came to a stop and stared at her in the mirror, something in her voice catching him. She was smoothing her hands down her sides and looking at the white carpet of the salon. Her mouth had gone tight.

'Do you like it?' he asked, suddenly tense for reasons he couldn't explain. 'Because, if you do, tell me.'

'If it's not right, it's not right,' she said expressionlessly. 'I can try on another.'

Her capitulation should have eased him, but it didn't. If anything, the tension inside him wound tighter. He didn't like that note in her voice. It sounded…passive.

Remind you of anyone?

The tension pulled tight as a bowstring.

Of course it did. She sounded like his mother trying to placate his father.

A kernel of ice sat in his gut.

He glanced down at the designer kneeling at Matilda's feet. 'I need a couple of minutes alone with my fiancée, please.'

The woman nodded and rose to her feet. 'Certainly, Mr Cardinali.'

There was a small silence after she'd gone, heavy in the carpeted luxury of the salon.

'If you don't like it, you don't have to wear it,' he said, curling his hands into fists and shoving them into his pockets. 'Choose another.'

'You said it was ordinary. And I know you don't want ordinary.' Her lashes rose, her grey eyes full of an understanding he didn't want to see. 'This is important to you, Enzo. I know that.'

Soothing him, that was what she was doing. Giving into him, the way his mother had always done with his father. As if what she wanted hadn't been important. But then, for his father it hadn't been.

He'd always been much too interested in the power he'd once had and then the power he'd lost.

Selfish. Just like you.

The ice in his gut spread outward.

Yes, his mother had always been right about that. He *was* his father's son. He was selfish and single-minded, and why not?

He'd never got what he needed from his father, because his father had never been interested in giving it to him. And his mother, well, she'd been honest at least. She'd told him up front that she didn't want anything from him, and then had made it plain that he wasn't going to get anything from her simply by removing herself from his life.

If there was one lesson he'd learned it was that he had to go out and get what he wanted himself. So he had. He'd built his company on the back of that self-ishness, built his own kingdom.

And now he was building his own family.

At Matilda's expense.

His breath caught as he remembered her in the library the night of their engagement party a week earlier. Of the way she'd cupped his face in her hands, her gaze fierce on his as she'd told him she wanted him exactly the way he was. And he'd felt his chest go tight at the look in her eyes.

She'd meant every word she said.

No one had ever said that to him before. No one had simply looked at him the way she had and accepted him for who and what he was, not given all his flaws—and he had so many of those.

And she hadn't demanded anything in return. Hadn't wanted him to give her anything at all. There had been no selfishness in her.

So he'd taken her hard up against those book-cases, the simple gift of her acceptance opening up something inside him he hadn't been able to leash. He'd thought it was only about giving her pleasure in return, but it hadn't been. There had been a hunger inside him, a demand. A need.

He didn't know what it was he wanted from her

but, in that moment, even physical pleasure hadn't seemed enough, though he'd made her promise that it would be.

Now she was standing there in the gown that he knew she liked and she was so achingly beautiful.

The gown was high-necked, demure almost, but the ivory silk made her skin glow and when she had her hair loose, like now, the red curls burned like fire against the pale fabric. The back of the dress wasn't quite so demure, however, plunging down almost to the swell of her delicious bottom, showing off her elegant spine.

She didn't need any further adornments.

She was breath-taking all on her own.

So why do you insist on turning her into your trophy?

'You're stunning,' he said hoarsely. 'The most beautiful thing I've ever seen.'

Her lashes fluttered, as if he'd taken her by surprise, and she turned around, her gaze meeting his. There was colour in her cheeks, a pretty pink, and it made her eyes glow. 'But, Enzo, I thought you—'

'Wear the dress.'

A crease appeared between her brows. 'Why?'

'Because you like it. Because you're beautiful in it. And because I don't need grand.'

You just need her.

His chest felt tight, aching, and the kernel of ice in his gut had put out roots, sending freezing tendrils through his body, wrapping around his heart.

He didn't want to need her. He didn't want to feel

anything for her. But he did. He cared about her. He cared because he knew he would crush that generous, warm spirit of hers. Because he knew himself. His mother was right—he was too like his father. He was nothing but selfish, caring only about what he wanted.

After all, he'd ended up driving his mother away because he'd wanted to prove to her that she didn't need alcohol to be happy. Or a throne. Or even a country. That they were together as a family and that that was all that had mattered.

But his mother had seen the real truth under all that justification.

He'd been ripped away from everything he'd ever known and he'd been desperate for reassurance, a pathetic black hole of need for attention.

He hadn't cared about her unhappiness. All that had mattered to him was his own pain, so he'd acted without even a single thought about how it would hurt her.

And it had broken his family apart.

Yes, he knew himself. He would do the same with Matilda and Simon too.

The crease between Matilda's brows deepened and she picked up her silken skirts in one hand, moving over to him. 'What's wrong?' The concern in her eyes cut him to the bone. 'If it's the dress, I can easily change it.' She was very close, her sweet scent all around him, the ivory silk of the gown accentuating her curves and making her skin look smooth and touchable.

'Don't,' he said roughly. 'Don't contort yourself into doing what I want just to placate me.'

She blinked. 'I'm not placating you.'

'You are. You liked that dress, and yet as soon I said I wanted something else you were okay with that.'

She lifted one shoulder, her mouth softening. 'It's just a dress, Enzo.'

'Dio,' he said, suddenly harsh. 'This isn't about the damn dress.'

'Then what is it about?'

She was so calm, her steady gaze unflinching. She'd been like that the night in the library, taking his ridiculous, inarticulate fury at himself and simply accepting it. And somehow turning it into white-hot passion.

He didn't know how she did that. He didn't know why seeing her in this gown made his heart ache with a pain that reached right down inside him, wrapped around him and wouldn't let go.

'I don't want you to deny yourself simply because it's not what I want,' he said through gritted teeth. 'I want you to be happy.'

Something flickered across her face, too fast for him to see what it was. 'I am happy.'

Enzo moved, pulling his hands from his pockets and putting them on her hips, tugging her towards him. 'Are you?' he demanded, because suddenly this was important. No, it was *vital.* 'Are you happy, *cara*?'

'Yes,' she said, her hands coming to rest over his. 'Of course I'm happy.'

But he'd seen the flicker behind that level gaze of hers. It had quickly been masked yet he'd seen it nonetheless.

His hands tightened on her hips as he searched her lovely face. 'Why are you lying to me, Matilda?'

'I'm not lying.' This time there was no flicker in her eyes and, when she lifted her hands to his chest, there was only heat there. 'Believe me.'

She rose up on tiptoes and brushed her mouth over his, and still he couldn't shake the sense that somehow she was only telling him what he wanted to hear.

Those tendrils of ice wound through his heart, slowly freezing him where he stood, and even the heat of her mouth wasn't enough to melt them.

Because he knew she couldn't be happy if she was forever bending herself to do what he wanted, the way his mother had with his father. And she *would* bend herself and not think twice about it simply because she was a loving, generous woman. Her aunt and uncle knew that, and Enzo suspected that St George had known it too; that was why he'd taken advantage of her the way he had.

The way Enzo himself had.

Yes, she'd bend. Until one day she wouldn't be able to bend any further and then she'd break. And he would be the one who'd broken her. He would destroy her, as he'd destroyed his own family.

You can't do it. You can't marry her.

The truth of it sank down inside him like a stone.

He wanted her to be happy because she mattered to him. But she could never be happy with him. In the end she'd contort so much she might as well have stayed in the box her aunt and uncle had made for her.

He could never do that to her. She was too important.

Clearly sensing his lack of response, Matilda slowly drew back. 'Enzo?'

There was only concern in her misty grey eyes. For him.

You don't deserve it. You don't deserve her.

No, he knew that. Perhaps he'd always known it.

'I need to get back to the office,' he said, knowing he sounded cold, yet not able to mask it. 'Get the dress.'

Then he turned around and walked out of the salon, leaving her standing there in the gown she was never going to wear.

Because he wasn't going to marry her after all.

Matilda couldn't settle the whole day after she'd got back from the bridal salon. Enzo's strange behaviour had disturbed her. The way he'd gone from being his usual dictatorial self to suddenly being concerned about whether she liked the dress or not, and then telling her that he didn't want her denying herself in order to make him happy, was worrying.

He'd never bothered to ask about her happiness before and what had prompted it, she didn't know. But it was the way he'd walked out, an almost blank expression on his face, that had bothered her the most.

She couldn't get it out of her head.

She spent the rest of the day with Simon, putting him to bed later that evening, before going to the library and settling herself on the couch with a book, waiting until Enzo got home.

She was tired, and he must have been very, *very* late, because the next thing she knew she opened her eyes to find him standing next to the couch in the process of pulling one of the soft, red cashmere throws over her.

Matilda blinked. 'Sorry,' she said thickly, pushing herself up. 'I must have fallen asleep.'

Enzo said nothing, merely turning away and moving back over to the fireplace, coming to a stop with his back to her.

There was something tense in his posture that made the unease she'd been feeling all day deepen even further.

'What is it?' she asked, clutching at the throw. 'I didn't get the dress in the end. I thought you might—'

'I can't marry you, Matilda.'

She stared at his still figure, cold shock washing through her. 'What?'

'I can't marry you,' he repeated, his voice heavy with finality. 'I'm sorry, but I can't.'

Something cold slid between her ribs like a cold, wickedly sharp blade. 'I...don't understand.'

Enzo slowly turned to look at her, the expression on his face icy and hard, the flame extinguished completely in his golden eyes. 'You need more than I can give you, *cara*. You need someone who will make you truly happy. And I am not that man.'

'No,' she said blankly, refusing to take it in. 'No, I told you that I was happy. I mean, I am happy—'

'Matilda.' His voice cut through hers like a knife. 'You lied. I could see it in your eyes.'

Her throat closed as a gulf opened up inside her. 'You promised,' she said thickly, pushing herself up off the couch, her hands shaking. 'You promised you wouldn't let me go. You promised me, Enzo.'

Pain flickered through his golden eyes, the ice melting a little. 'I know I did. But I can't keep that promise any more. I have to let you and Simon go.'

She was moving towards him, crossing the distance and standing right in front of him. 'Why?' she demanded, a sudden, hot anger burning through her. 'Why? Because you can't make me happy? That's the only reason? I told you that what you could give me was enough, Enzo, and I meant it.'

'It's *not* enough.' Something sparked in his eyes, a ghost of his usual ferocity. 'What I can give you is not enough. Sex and money are not enough! You need more than that, Matilda. *Dio*, you deserve more.'

'That's not all you're giving me.' She took another step closer, looking up at him into his beautiful eyes. 'You're giving me a family. A place to belong. I'm yours because I want to be. I don't *want* anything else.'

Enzo reached out all of a sudden, his fingers curling around her upper arms, his palms scorching her through the cotton of her T-shirt, his face a blaze of intensity. 'You don't understand, *cara*. If I keep you, I will crush you. You'll end up contorting yourself, bending yourself like you did in the bridal salon today. Trying to make yourself into what I want.'

'I won't.'

'You will. That's all you've been doing your whole life.'

She trembled, a shudder of realisation going through her. Because, yes, that was exactly what she'd been doing. With her aunt and uncle. With Henry.

And you'll do it with him too. And not because you have to but because you love him.

She tried to swallow, but her throat felt too thick. 'I don't mind,' she forced out. 'I don't mind doing that for you.'

His gaze was steady, fierce now. 'But I do. I won't have you turning into my mother. I won't bend you so much that you break. I already broke the family I had and I won't break another. Because eventually I will, *cara*. I will.'

She blinked. 'What do you mean, you "broke" your family?'

'After we were exiled, I was desperately unhappy. I felt isolated. My father was always out visiting supporters and my mother was so deep in her own misery she had nothing to give me.' A muscle flicked in his jaw. 'I told you that I poured out all the alcohol in our cupboards because I was trying to help her. But…that's not why I did it. The truth is that I did it because I wanted her to look at me, to pay attention to me. I didn't care about her or her unhappiness. Only my unhappiness mattered; only what I wanted was important. And so she left, Matilda. She left because of me, because of my selfishness. And it broke our family apart. It destroyed it.'

'You can't possibly take the blame for that. You were only young. And if she was drinking—'

'I've made my decision,' he interrupted. 'And it is final.'

Her eyes stung, full of tears. 'But… I love you, Enzo.'

Something like anguish crossed his face, bright and fleeting. Then he opened his hands and released her. 'And that is why I have to let you go.'

Enzo felt as if someone had put a hand around his heart and was squeezing tight. He could barely get a breath.

She loved him. *Dio*, why did that feel like the worst betrayal of all?

She was standing there in front of him, wearing jeans and a T-shirt—nothing special, yet she somehow blazed like the sun. Her hair was piled in a loose bun on her head, flaming and beautiful, her skin was like fresh cream and he wanted to pull her to him, crush her mouth under his.

But her eyes had gone as dark as rainclouds and there was pain in them. 'Why?' Her voice had gone husky. 'Why does love make any difference?'

'Because it does.' He curled his hands into fists at his sides. 'Because love means you want more from me and I can't give it to you.' His chest heaved as he tried to draw in a breath. 'I will never be able to give it to you.'

She slowly shook her head, silver glinting in her lovely eyes. 'I didn't ask you for more. I told you I wanted you as you are. And I do. I love you as you are.'

'And that's the problem, *cara*. I don't want you to love me as I am.' He tried to cut himself off from the pain growing inside him, tried to make himself ice. 'I'm not worth it. I'm selfish and manipulative. I'm single-minded and I'm cruel. And I don't want to change. I won't.'

A tear slid down the side of her nose, leaving a trail of silver, and it felt as if that fist was squeezing his heart into nothing but a bloody pulp.

This shouldn't hurt so much.

He didn't understand it.

'I don't want you to change,' she said softly. 'And I never asked you to.'

'I know you didn't. But it's too late anyway.' He tried to make the words sharp and cold, but there was a rough edge of pain he couldn't quite hide. 'I've made up my mind. You can't stay with me. I won't let you.'

She blinked hard, as if she was holding back her tears. 'Okay. I get it now.' Her throat moved as swallowed. 'I know why you never came after me all those years ago.'

The change of subject caught him off-guard. 'What do you mean?'

'I mean, you were too afraid then and you're too afraid now.'

His gut lurched. 'No,' he said harshly, trying to ignore it. 'I was never—'

'No,' she cut him off, anger suddenly blazing in her eyes. 'I don't want to hear your excuses. I can handle you letting me go, but what the hell do I tell our son? That his papa didn't want him any more? That he was too afraid of love to keep him?'

The pain deepened, broadened, inside him. Because of course there was someone else in this utter mess he'd created whom he had to consider. Someone else who would suffer because of him.

'I'll tell Simon myself…that situations change and that he's better off with his mother. I will visit him, though. You can count on that.'

'And I'm sure that will make him feel better,' Matilda said, her voice caustic. 'When he's ripped away from what he thought was his home for a second time.'

Anguish twisted inside Enzo and there was a part of him dimly amazed by how much it hurt even now, when his heart was nothing but bloody pulp.

Why did he only realise what he was destroying when it was too late?

'Simon's better off without me,' he said, harsh and cold. 'I'll do nothing but turn him into a carbon copy of myself. Of my father.' He turned away abruptly, heading for the door, needing to get away from her. 'I'll book you and Simon flights to London tomorrow. You can stay in my Knightsbridge house for as long as you like.'

He'd reached the door by the time her voice came

from behind him, cracked and raw-sounding. 'I never thought that in the end you would be the one to run away, Enzo.'

For a second it felt as though she'd shot him.

But only for a second.

Then he walked out of the door without a backward glance.

CHAPTER TWELVE

ISOLA SACRA, THE island Enzo had bought from Henry St George, with its terraced gardens and white stone villa, was beautiful. Peaceful too, with the deep, blue sea all around, the waves lapping against the rocky cliffs.

There was a perfect little beach at the base of the cliffs beneath the villa where a boathouse had been built to house the small yacht Enzo had bought for his son.

One day Simon would come here to sail.

But it wouldn't be today.

Enzo had spent the past week on the island cleaning up the ruins of his wedding, paying the people who needed to be paid and making his excuses to those who needed them, while ignoring those who didn't.

The media of course made a big fuss, but he tried to keep the glare of the camera on himself and not on Matilda or Simon. His staff had reported that they were safe in his house in London—at least until they'd disappeared a couple of days later.

At the same time, he'd received a text from Matilda telling him she and Simon were heading out of town and that he needn't try to look for them. It was easier for her to remain out of the public eye that way.

Everything in him had wanted to pay some people to go and find her, track her down to make sure she was safe, but he didn't. Instead, he let her go.

It was the hardest thing he'd ever had to do.

The second hardest thing was being on this island, wandering the empty halls of the villa he'd built for his family and knowing that it was going to stay empty for ever.

He'd come back here, determined to have the home he'd wanted anyway—because he'd paid for it, by God. He'd sacrificed *everything* for it.

Yet it didn't feel like home.

All it felt like was a house with no one in it.

A throne with no kingdom.

He didn't know what to do with himself.

Every night he came into the room he'd planned for himself and Matilda, and he lay in the big, low four-poster bed hung with gauzy curtains patterned with jasmine flowers. For her scent.

And he lay awake, staring at the canopy above his head, a burning coal in his chest, painful and hot, eating him alive.

Nothing was going to put it out.

In the mornings, when he rose gritty-eyed from the bed from lack of sleep, and he came out onto the terrace to eat his breakfast, he kept seeing that beach where he'd been supposed to teach his son to sail.

And it made him want to smash something.

So he got up from the table, went into the bed-room, tore the jasmine-patterned curtains from the bed and ripped them apart from end to end.

Which naturally didn't make him feel any better.

One morning the sound of helicopter rotors echoed in the air, and when he came out onto the ter-race to see who was daring to interrupt his exile he saw his brother's tall figure making his way through the gardens to the house.

Enzo waited on the terrace until Dante finally stepped out and then he said, 'Go away, Dante. I have nothing to say to you.'

'And good morning to you.' Dante ignored him, coming over to the table and pulling up a chair. 'You look like hell, if you don't mind me saying.'

'Didn't you hear what I said?' Enzo demanded.

'Of course. I'm just choosing to ignore it.'

'Dante—'

'Enzo,' Dante interrupted. 'Sit down and shut up.'

There wasn't anything else to do and, as he didn't have the energy to put up a fight, Enzo sat down and shut up.

'Now,' Dante said, pouring himself some of the thick black coffee that stood in the carafe on the table. 'Isn't it time you stopped punishing yourself?'

Enzo blinked at him. He'd expected his brother to say many things, but it wasn't that. 'What?'

'Papa was a bastard. And, yes, I know why Mama left and what she said to you. About how you poured out her wine—I'm afraid to say she preferred vodka—and how she told you that you were just like him. But she was wrong. You're nothing like him, Enzo, and you never were.'

'But I—'

'Did you ever put a throne before anyone?'

'No, but I—'

'Did you ever ignore your own child so completely you made him feel like he didn't exist?'

'Dante—'

'You were restless and impatient, and moody and volatile, sure. But you know what set you apart from him?'

'Control,' Enzo said flatly, finally getting a word in. 'I controlled my emotions, unlike him.'

'No, Enzo.' Dante's voice was unexpectedly gentle. 'What set you apart from him was that you cared. You cared about people. You cared about Mama. And you cared about me.'

Enzo sat there, feeling as if he'd been turned to stone. 'No, that's a lie. It was myself I cared about. I didn't care that she was—'

'Drinking herself to death because she was unhappy?' Dante reached over, picked up his coffee cup and took a sip. 'Mama had her issues, it's true. But she didn't need to put them all on you or blame you for them. And she did, Enzo. You were sixteen and you needed her. And she wasn't there for you. You didn't deserve to be abandoned the way she abandoned you. The way they *both* abandoned you. And it wasn't your fault.'

'I didn't think it was.' *Liar.*

Dante's dark eyes were very direct. 'Didn't you? Cancelling your wedding? Sitting all alone here in this lovely villa? Letting go of Matilda and Simon, when anyone with eyes in their heads can see that they were the centre of your world?'

Enzo couldn't speak. The words stuck in his throat, the burning in his heart taking everything. 'I had to,' he eventually forced out. 'I would have only caused them hurt. I would have broken them the way I broke our family.'

'Why? Because you poured out Mama's wine? Because you believed her when she told you that you were like Papa?' Dante snorted. 'Please. You'll have to think of better excuses than that. Now, if you really want to be like Papa, then by all means sit here sulking and thinking about everything you've lost. But there's a beautiful girl out there who, if I'm not much mistaken, loves you. And every day you sit here is another day that you're causing her pain.' His brother raised a brow. 'So what's it to be? Here's a hint for you: a truly unselfish man would give her the choice, not decide what's best for her himself. Especially not if that decision was based solely on fear.'

The words shuddered down Enzo's spine like an axe blade biting deep into a tree trunk.

She'd told him she loved him and he'd simply shut down even harder because he hadn't wanted to hear it.

He hadn't wanted to know.

He hadn't wanted to look inside his own heart and examine why letting her go had hurt so much. Why, at the end, he'd been so afraid himself.

You love her too.

The hot coal burned in his chest. 'I don't deserve her,' he said hoarsely. 'I will never deserve her.'

Dante sipped his coffee and looked at him over the rim of his cup. 'Maybe you won't. But what she deserves is the chance to find out for herself.'

Another shudder went through him, deep and hard.

Yes, she did deserve that. And so much more. She deserved to have *everything* she wanted, and that included love.

She'd loved him as he was; she'd never asked him to change. She'd given him everything and never asked him for anything in return.

But, by God, she should have.

And now it was time for him to give back to her. With interest.

Enzo put his hands on the table top and he pushed himself out of his chair.

Dante raised a brow. 'What are you doing?'

But Enzo was already moving. 'If you don't want to spend the next week on this island by yourself, you'd better come with me now.'

Dante put down his cup. 'Why?'

'Because I'm taking your helicopter.'

Enzo's house in Knightsbridge was lovely, but Matilda knew she couldn't stay there. There had been some media attention, once the news that the wedding had been cancelled had hit, but his staff had been very good at fending off the worst of it.

But still, she didn't want to stay.

She didn't want to be anywhere that reminded her of him.

Simon kept asking why Papa wasn't with them, but she kept going back to what Enzo had told Simon the morning they'd left: that she and Simon would be going on a small holiday to visit England while Papa stayed in Italy working. He'd see Papa again soon enough.

Her son seemed to accept this though he kept talking about the island and the boat that Enzo had promised to teach him to sail in, and all the sandcastles he was going to build when they got 'home'.

It made tears clog in Matilda's throat.

She hired a car in the end—even though Enzo's house had a garage full of them that she could have borrowed—and drove out of London, thinking that perhaps she'd take Simon to her aunt and uncle's place. But when she got there she found the house shut up and empty. A neighbour told her that her aunt and uncle had gone on an extended cruise and wouldn't be back for at least six weeks.

It hurt that they hadn't told her. But then, they never told her what they were doing—as if, once she'd married Henry, it was out of sight, out of mind.

After that, she actually called Henry, thinking that perhaps she and Simon could visit and maybe stay. But he didn't answer his phone.

There was nowhere for her to go after that, nowhere for her to stay.

She and Simon had no one.

She stayed the night in a run-down hotel beside the motorway, which was all she could afford as she was trying to use her own money and not Enzo's, but Simon didn't like it. He was grumpy and restless, and he didn't want to go to bed. He wanted 'a long mis-understandable story' first. It took her a while to figure out that apparently Enzo had been telling him long bedtime stories in Italian that Simon hadn't understood but that he really liked hearing anyway.

'I miss Papa,' he said as Matilda tucked him into bed.

'So do I,' she replied, her voice husky as she smoothed the bed clothes over her son, staring down into golden eyes so familiar, they broke her heart. 'So do I.'

Once Simon was asleep, she sat on the run-down, musty-smelling couch and got out her phone, unable to stop herself from looking at the news sites, searching for any story about him. Just to see what he was doing. But, following the fuss over the wedding cancelation, any gossip seemed to have calmed down. Or maybe Enzo had just exerted his influence to silence it.

Her heart ached. Everything ached.

It should have made it easier that she hadn't been the one to run this time, but it didn't. If anything, it was worse. Because she'd told him that she loved him and he'd simply thrown that back in her face.

Love hadn't been enough in the end.

But she wasn't going to beat herself up like she had in the past, or settle for any scraps he was going to throw her, because if that had been true she would have begged Enzo that night. Got down on her knees and pleaded for him to keep her.

But she hadn't. She'd walked away from him with her head held high.

This time she hadn't been the one who was afraid. That was all on him.

There was a knock on the door and Matilda's heart seized.

It wasn't that late, but still it was dark outside, and she wasn't expecting anyone. Who on earth could it be?

Simon was asleep in the bedroom so she quickly went over to the door and pulled it shut. Then she cast around for something large and heavy, just in case.

The knock sounded again and, failing to find a weapon, she crept over to the door, her heartbeat shuddering inside her chest, and put her eye to the peephole.

A tall, broad man stood outside, staring at her, and his golden eyes seemed to see straight through the peephole and into her.

Enzo.

A wave of fury washed through her and she'd flung open the door before she had a chance to think straight.

'How dare you?' she said in a shaking voice. 'How dare you come back here and—?'

He didn't let her finish. He merely reached out, cupped her face between his big palms and kissed her. And he kissed her. And he kissed her.

And then he urged her back into the room and kicked the door shut behind him.

Then he raised his mouth from hers and looked down at her, all fierce, predatory claim. 'You were right, Matilda,' he said roughly. 'You were right about all of it. I thought letting you go was the right thing to do, that you and Simon needed to be protected from my selfishness. I'd already broken one family. I didn't want to break another. But...' His fingers were hot on her skin and her heartbeat wouldn't slow down. 'The only person I was protecting was myself. *Cara*, I didn't want to be like my father, and yet I ended up proving my mother right and being exactly like him in the end. I was afraid and I let my fear be more important than the fact that you loved me.' His voice got even rougher. 'But it shouldn't be.'

Her hands pressed against his chest, her throat tight and sore. She couldn't breathe for the ache in her heart. Could barely understand what he was even saying. 'Is that why you came back? To tell me you were afraid?'

His eyes were bright, blazing gold. 'No. I came back to tell you that I love you, Matilda. That you are more important than my fear, than all my money, than my lost kingdom. You're more important than anything on this earth, except perhaps my son.' He kissed her, suddenly hard and fierce. 'I'm yours. I was yours the moment I saw you on that island. Body and soul.'

He was holding her so tightly, his heat warming up the cold places inside her. *All* the cold places.

She shivered, curling her fingers into the cotton of his shirt, her heart feeling far too full and large for her chest. 'I will never leave you,' she said fiercely, holding onto him. 'Understand me? There's nothing you do that will make me walk away from you again.'

His gaze burned. 'Don't worry, *cara*. I wouldn't let you anyway. You're mine now. Truly mine. And I never let go of what's mine.' He gripped her a little tighter, fitting her more closely against him, as if he could make her part of him. 'I think you're what I've been wanting my whole life. Searching for and never finding, until I saw you on that island.'

Tears stung her eyes, but they were good tears this time. 'Enzo...'

'I'm afraid,' he said softly. 'Don't let me break you. Don't let me destroy what we have.'

'You won't break me and you won't destroy anything.' She pressed her hand above his heart. 'You didn't destroy your family, Enzo. That wasn't your fault. You're not your mother or your father, and I'm not my uncle and aunt. Yes, we'll have difficult times, but don't forget that we have something they never did. We have love. And it's love that will get us through those difficult times, and it's love that will heal us afterwards.'

He smiled suddenly, a fierce and beautiful smile, making her heart turn over and over inside her chest. 'You're very strong, Summer mine. Very wise. I knew that right from the start.'

And she smiled back because she couldn't help

herself. Because he'd said that name and it didn't hurt. It made her feel nothing but joy.

'Of course I'm strong,' she said. 'Pressure doesn't crush me. It just produces diamonds.'

His smile deepened, holding all the warmth and sunlight that she'd remembered from long ago. 'Which reminds me. There's something I want to ask you.' Then he let her go and, before she could say a word, he got down on one knee and held out his hand to her. 'Will you do me the honour of becoming my wife, Matilda St George?'

The tears returned and this time no amount of blinking would hold them back. 'Yes,' she said thickly, her heart full to overflowing. 'Yes, I will.'

'Good,' Enzo said. 'Because you've still got my ring.'

And Matilda laughed.

At that moment, the door of the bedroom opened and a small, black-haired, golden-eyed boy put his head around the door. 'Papa?'

Enzo stood up and grinned at his son. *'Buona sera, Simon.'*

And he opened his arms.

EPILOGUE

ENZO STROKED HIS hands down his wife's side, curving them over her rounded stomach. A warm summer wind was coming through the open doors of their bedroom, carrying with it the scent of the sea and the sound of their son laughing as he played in the gardens below with one of the island staff's sons.

A deep feeling of peace filled Enzo…the hungry part of his soul had gone quiet.

But not too quiet.

Matilda was smiling up at him, her red curls in a halo around her head in fiery contrast to the white of the pillow, and he could feel himself getting hard for her. Again.

'You should probably go down,' she said, sliding a hand over his bare shoulder. 'Simon will be getting impatient.'

Enzo was going to take his son for his first sailing lesson, and to say that Simon was excited was an understatement.

'He can wait a minute or two longer,' Enzo murmured, bending to kiss her stomach where his daughter slept, waiting to be born. 'We're not going to have a lot of time to ourselves once this one arrives.'

Matilda's gaze turned smoky. 'Well, maybe he can wait a little longer then. But it had better be more than a minute or two.'

Enzo gave her a wicked look. 'For you, Summer mine, it'll be five at least.'

This time she laughed and tightened her grip on him.

And it was more than five.

With smiles and laughter, and much love, they turned it into for ever.

* * * * *

*If you enjoyed Jackie Ashenden's
debut for Presents,*
Demanding His Hidden Heir,
*look out for the next instalment in
her Shocking Italian Heirs duet:*
Claiming His One-Night Child,
coming soon!

*And why not explore these other
Secret Heirs of Billionaires stories?*

The Sheikh's Secret Baby
by Sharon Kendrick
The Sicilian's Secret Son
by Angela Bissell
Claimed for the Sheikh's Shock Son
by Carol Marinelli
Shock Heir for the King
by Clare Connelly

Available now!

#3737 THE ARGENTINIAN'S BABY OF SCANDAL
One Night With Consequences
by Sharon Kendrick

Housekeeper Tara is always professional. Until her billionaire boss, Lucas, looks at her with an intensity she just can't resist... Only now this innocent Cinderella has the task of flying to New York to tell him about the scandalous consequence!

#3738 THE MAID'S SPANISH SECRET
Secret Heirs of Billionaires
by Dani Collins

Sweet Poppy shouldn't have succumbed to aristocrat Rico's seduction, but his forbidden touch was all consuming... And it had a nine-month consequence! Now Rico's on her doorstep, demanding his hidden daughter and determined to make Poppy his wife!

#3739 AN HEIR FOR THE WORLD'S RICHEST MAN
by Maya Blake

To secure his latest deal, Joao needs his right-hand woman, Saffron. But a one-off, emotionally charged night together leads the tension between them to skyrocket...and then Joao discovers that Saffron is pregnant!

#3740 CONTRACTED AS HIS CINDERELLA BRIDE
Conveniently Wed!
by Heidi Rice

The perfect summer Ally spent with billionaire Dominic was unforgettable. But now Ally's a struggling courier, and she's stunned when her latest delivery brings her to Dominic's door. Yet what's even more shocking is his marriage proposal!